PLANNING FOR LOVE

Mia Bowman has a plan for everything. Right now, her plan is to go to Crete, leaving all family distractions behind, and finish her first novel. This is her dream, and she has its achievement scheduled down to the last minute. Then she meets the handsome Alex, and starts to wonder whether everything in life can be planned for. Soon, Mia must decide whether to stick to her schedule or follow her heart . . .

Books by Sarah Purdue
in the Linford Romance Library:

STANDING THE TEST OF TIME

SARAH PURDUE

PLANNING
FOR LOVE

Complete and Unabridged

LINFORD
Leicester

First published in Great Britain in 2016

First Linford Edition
published 2017

*A catalogue record for this book is available
from the British Library.*

ISBN 978–1–4448–3294–5

Published by
F. A. Thorpe (Publishing)
Anstey, Leicestershire

Set by Words & Graphics Ltd.
Anstey, Leicestershire
Printed and bound in Great Britain by
T. J. International Ltd., Padstow, Cornwall

This book is printed on acid-free paper

1

The hot air hit Mia and she hoped that her tablet would be able to cope with the high temperatures. She switched it on as soon as the warning signs were no longer visible and then checked her itinerary on her tablet against her wristwatch, which she had set to Crete local time. She was twelve minutes behind schedule but she felt she could probably catch up at the luggage carousel. Mia had spent much of the four and a half hour flight rehearsing her approach to retrieving her luggage. Her suitcase, whilst navy blue in colour and like every other suitcase, had a bright yellow ribbon tied around it to make it easily identifiable. Mia had decided that she would take up her position near to where the luggage entered the public area. Once she had spotted her luggage she would keep track of it around the conveyer belt and then seeing a gap, make her move.

Forty minutes later and Mia had to concede that it was impossible to plan for every eventuality no matter how hard she tried. The tannoy had announced a short delay to the baggage reclaim due to the mechanical failure of the lift which removed suitcases from the plane. The reassuring voice had claimed that the problem would be fixed momentarily. In ten more minutes she would have to go to plan B which involved sending an email to the taxi company that she had booked to take her to her accommodation, to warn them that she would in fact be late. Mia hated to be late.

The other passengers were becoming equally restless; clearly everyone was ready to leave the stuffy airport and begin their holiday. A grinding noise signalled that the belt was starting to move and the crowd, as one, surged forward. Men stood elbow to elbow and women hung around with trollies, waiting to relieve their other halves of a suitcase to ready them for the next one. Children of all ages lounged around and moaned about the heat, lack of food and drink and the desire to get into the nearest swimming pool. Mia felt an instant kinship to them, not that she wanted the same thing. She wanted peace and quiet and some space, after which she would track down the nearest pint of milk and make herself a much longed for cup of tea.

The wall of men was solid; when one dropped back to hand over a suitcase the gap was instantly filled by another tall, wide man. Mia glanced around her and noticed that other single travellers were not even trying to retrieve their luggage. They had clearly resigned themselves to a long wait. Mia was having none of this and since she did not want to have to revert to Plan C, launched herself into the wall of men with her angular elbows pointing outwards. This was a trick she had learnt out of necessity, since she was only five feet tall, and it had turned out to be the only way to get to the bar if you wanted a drink.

There was some resistance, so Mia had

to revert to 'accidentally' standing on the odd sandaled foot — but since they also seemed to be wearing socks with said sandals (surely a cardinal sin in anyone's book), she decided it might bring their own attention to the inappropriateness of their footwear combination. Mia caught a glimpse of a yellow ribbon on the far side of the carousel and readied herself. She grabbed the handle ... and found herself moving with the suitcase around the carousel. She knew that she should have paid more attention to the weight and paid for an extra bag to divide it up; she was, after all, planning to stay for six months.

Now the elbows and toe-crunches as she progressed were no longer tactical, but she soon stopped apologising and started to wonder if anyone was planning to help her. It she carried on with her forward momentum she would disappear through the rubber curtain and find herself back out on the tarmac. She felt a hand grab her elbow, whether to stop her forward motion or to prevent personal injury, she wasn't sure. With one swift movement she found herself standing behind the wall of men and her rescuer wheeling her suitcase towards her.

'Here you are, Ma'am,' a distinctly American voice said, before letting go of the handle. 'Are you alright?'

'Yes, thank you. For a moment there I thought I was going to end up going back through to baggage handling.'

She smiled and for the first time looked up into her rescuer's face. He was tall — but then, everyone was tall from where she stood. He looked a little bohemian, with a coloured, well-worn scarf draped around his neck and a crumpled white linen shirt. She put his age at the top end of thirties, maybe early forties. He had a broad grin and an open face. In the pocket of his carry-on bag, Mia could see a paperback sticking out. A fellow reader was always a good sign. He held out his hand to her and Mia shook it.

'Parker Edwards. And you are?'

'Mia, Mia Bowman.'

Mia smiled at his directness.

5

'Can I help you find your way?' he asked. Mia shook her head.

'I have a taxi booked, thank you. It should be waiting for me in the arrivals hall.' There was a pause. 'Well the driver, not the taxi, obviously.'

Mia was rewarded with a booming laugh that made her jump just a little.

'Let me take you there, this place is a bit of a maze.'

'Are you a local?' Mia asked, as they started to move with the steady flow of people. Parker had insisted on pulling her suitcase. He himself only had a small carry-on bag, which piqued her curiosity.

'For a few months a year, I guess you could say I am. Are you here on vacation?' he asked, his eyes studying her so closely that Mia had to look away.

'A working one, here for six months, if all goes to plan.'

'Me too.' He grinned again and then pointed with his free hand. 'This is you?' he said. Mia followed his pointed finger to a man holding a sign with 'Mia Bowman' written on it in capital letters.

'Yes, it is. Thank you again for your help,' she said, taking hold of her suitcase.

'See you around, Mia, Mia Bowman,' Parker said, before disappearing through the crowds and out into the daylight.

'Mia Bowman?' the driver asked.

'That's me,' she said, tearing her eyes away from the retreating figure of Parker Edwards, the first person she had met on her Greek adventure. Looking up at the driver, she was hit by a funny sensation in her belly. She blinked and the mirage did not disappear. He was not what she was expecting. He was young for a start — about her age, mid-twenties. He wasn't smoking the perpetual cigarette that seemed to signify a Greek man, and he was dressed in jeans and a black T-shirt with 'University College London', emblazoned across the front. And he was gorgeous! Mia had the sensation of butterflies in the pit of her stomach and felt sure she could hear a choir singing somewhere in the distance. Was that what everyone went on about when they talked about love at first sight? She quickly ran a hand surreptitiously across her mouth to check that she wasn't drooling.

'My name is Alessandro Nikolas, I am your driver. Let me take your case.'

His voice portrayed a glimmer of an accent, but if Mia had been at home in England, she would probably not have picked up on it.

'This way,' he said with a smile, seemingly oblivious to her staring — or maybe he was just used to it.

He started off towards the exit. Mia had to do a little jog to keep up. She kept her eyes firmly fixed on him so as not to lose him in the crowd, but she needn't have worried, as he paused every now and then to make sure she was still with him. Each time he stopped he flashed her a smile of white teeth, set against his tanned face. Not only was this man beautifully handsome but he had impeccable manners. She watched as he loaded her suitcase into the back of the car, marvelling at the lack of effort it seemed to take him to lift it up, and then watched as he held open the passenger side door. Mia was used to sitting in the back of taxis at home, but he was being such a gentleman that it seemed churlish to refuse. Of course, she had not met a taxi driver that she wanted to converse with on a long journey before now either.

They queued to exit the airport and wound their way through the tourist-clogged streets of Heraklion. Mia took it all in and gave herself an imaginary pat on the back for doing her research and picking Agios Nikolaos instead. Heraklion was definitely not her kind of place and definitely not the place she would find inspiration.

'You don't like what you see?' His voice startled her out of her self-congratulation.

'I'm sure it's a great place, if you like that kind of thing.' Sitting in the front, she realised, not only gave her a great view, it also gave her driver the opportunity to study her.

'And you don't?' he asked, and when she looked at him she could see a mischievous glint in his eyes.

'I probably shouldn't say this, but there are too many English tourists for me.' She smiled to show that she was half joking.

'It is an acquired taste, but with the economy like it is, I think we are all glad of the business.'

Mia smiled to herself. He was clearly a thoughtful man.

'Do you live here?' she asked. He laughed out loud; it was deep and warm, and Mia felt herself relax a little in his company.

'No, Miss Bowman. I live in Agios Nikolaos, not too far from where you are staying. In fact, my parents own a little taverna just a few streets away from your apartment. Perhaps when you are settled and refreshed you might come and enjoy supper with me?'

Mia felt her heart leap and she forced herself to look back out of the window to give herself a few moments to consider the invite.

'That's very kind, but ... ' Mia's mind returned to her schedule, created to encompass the whole six months. Having dinner with a taxi driver she had just met did not really feature.

'In Crete, we do not eat alone; it is bad for the digestion. And I think perhaps you will need to get your bearings? I can show you around a little if you would like?'

Mia thought for a moment. She wasn't here to be distracted, that was definitely not part of the plan. She'd had enough of distractions at home and had promised herself it would be different here. But dinner didn't have to mean a full-blown love affair, did it? Although she longed for peace and quiet, the thought of six months spent entirely on her own wasn't appealing either. She had allowed a certain amount of time for casual acquaintances, and besides, if Alessandro showed her round then she would be able to save some of the time she'd allocated to exploring.

'Ok, that would be lovely. What time?'

'About eight, if that gives you enough time to get settled?'

Mia mentally rearranged her schedule and nodded.

11

'Lovely.'

The car joined a main highway and Mia lost herself to the beautiful scenery and thoughts of what lay ahead.

2

Mia had unpacked and rearranged her room in the new apartment block that was to be called home. It seemed quiet when she arrived, which suited her. In fact, she had not seen a single other person, not along the corridors she had walked while getting to her room, and not out lounging by the pool that her balcony overlooked.

She had taken out one of her light summer dresses, found a plug socket for her travel iron, ironed out the inevitable packing creases and dressed. None of this had taken place, of course, until she had updated her schedule and texted various family and friends to say that she arrived safely.

Tomorrow, when she was sure she would have more to say, she would send a generic global email, to save time on repeating herself. She brushed out her shoulder-length, strawberry-blonde hair one more time and checked her watch. It was seven-thirty. Alessandro had said that his family's taverna was a five-minute walk from her apartment and had drawn her a quick map on the back of his taxi business card. If she left now she would have plenty of time to make sure she was in the right place and then have a quick wander round without risking being late.

★ ★ ★

The Nikolas family taverna was the kind of place Mia would have walked past at home. It had a huge, sun-bleached shade suspended from the front of the building and an eclectic selection of tables and chairs, many of which were propped up with folded beer coasters. It did not have the sea views of the restaurants by the many small fishing boats in the harbour, but it opened out onto one of many ancient squares with a small stone fountain at its heart. The square seemed quiet, no

14

English pubs or nightclubs here. A few locals seemed to be making their way home and some of the tavernas had early diners sitting outside enjoying the last of the setting sun.

An older couple were the only current customers at the Nikolas Taverna. They were sat on the very outside edge, sipping at their wine and trying not to look conspicuous. To Mia, they screamed, 'English, on holiday and trying our best to blend in.' She smiled at them as she walked past and they smiled back. With no sign of Alessandro, Mia stepped into the building part of the taverna. The light here was dim, and it took a moment for her eyes to adjust.

'You must be Mia,' a woman's voice said. She was taller than Mia, with ivory skin and brown hair. If Mia had to guess, she would have said the woman was in her fifties.

'Hi,' Mia said, shyly, holding out a hand. They both stared at it for a moment and then Mia found herself pulled into a quick hug.

'In Crete, we hug,' she said, with an apologetic shrug. 'Don't worry, you'll get used to it.' She added in a conspiratorial whisper, 'Alex asked me to keep an eye out for you. I suspected that you would not be on Grecian time yet.'

Mia looked at the clock above the bar in confusion. It showed just before eight. The woman laughed merrily.

'Oh, you are on time, my dear. It's just that in Greece, time is a very fluid thing. If you want a Greek family to be sat at the table by eight o'clock, you tell them that they need to be here by six.' With one arm around Mia's shoulders she steered her towards a series of linked tables at the back of the taverna.

'Of course, they would not believe you, since no one would consider eating their supper that early!'

She directed Mia to a chair at one end of the table. 'Alex will be here shortly, he had one final drop off at the airport. Now, what can I get you to drink?'

'Sparkling water, please,' Mia said.

'Always water, but what would you like

16

to *drink*?'

Mia couldn't be certain but she was sure that she had seen the same mischievous glint in Alessandro's eyes.

'Some wine, please. Rosé, if you have it?'

'I will bring you some meze to mop up some of the alcohol; it may be some time till we eat.'

'Thank you,' Mia said, feeling a bit confused. She was not sure who this woman was, although she guessed she was some relation of Alessandro's, and had she just said, it will be some time till *we* eat? That couldn't be right, could it? She mulled this over as her wine arrived with a dish of olives, some freshly baked bread and dips. Her stomach rumbled in appreciation. Perhaps it was a language thing? Often the little words which gave such meaning were the hardest to master. Mia told herself firmly to relax and embrace the different culture; this was one of the reasons she had come to Crete.

A figure walked into the taverna and was greeted by the woman with much hugging and kissing. He said something in Greek and then waved to Mia, having spotted her in her seat. He held her eye contact as he walked towards her and Mia was torn between looking away, which seemed the thing to do, and being completely intoxicated by his gaze.

'Mia, sorry I am late. The airport was very busy and my passengers had a lot of luggage.'

Mia smiled. 'I believe I am the one who is early.'

'You will get used to it,' he said with a laugh, before popping an olive into his mouth. 'You met my ma? I hope she didn't ask too many embarrassing questions.'

Mia took a sip of wine, taking in the information.

'No, not at all, she has been very welcoming.'

'She has a homing instinct for a fellow Brit.'

Mia couldn't help but raise an eyebrow, although the woman's colouring should have given it away, it was very

18

'English Rose'.

Alessandro's mother had arrived with a bottle of cold beer for her son, just as he finished speaking.

'I came to the island when I was eighteen, just out of school. Fell in love with the place, and Alex's father, and have been here ever since. You should watch yourself Mia. This island has magical powers, as do its men.'

'Ma!' Alex said with a shake of his head. 'Enough! Why do you torture the poor girl, she is our guest.'

Mia laughed, feeling surprisingly at home.

'The little that I have seen has certainly been beautiful, and I'm sure I will fall in love with Crete, but I am only here for six months and then I must go home.' She smiled up at the older woman but kept a sideways glance out for Alex's reaction.

'We'll see, we'll see,' the older woman said. 'My family call me Elisávet but you can call me Elizabeth if you prefer the English. You are always welcome here,

Mia, please consider yourself part of our family.'

Mia watched as the older woman's gaze flicked to her son and then she left to seat another couple who had come to eat.

'Sorry about that. My mother sometimes seems to have taken the worst from both her cultures.' Alex took a swig of his beer. 'So how is your apartment?' he asked, relaxing back into his chair and turning his attention fully to Mia, which she found a little unsettling.

'Seems quiet and clean. No complaints from me.'

Alex nodded but looked as if he did not agree.

'What?'

He shrugged casually. 'I think perhaps that is because you have not yet met your fellow tenants.'

Mia's heart sank, feeling a little of her positive attitude slipping. It was hard to plan for who the other people in your building were going to be.

'What's wrong with them?' she asked, even though she wasn't sure she wanted to know the answer.

'I am sure they are all lovely people.'

Mia rolled her eyes; this was like trying to get blood from a stone.

'But … ?'

'The apartment block is usually hired out by the holiday companies.'

Mia nodded. She knew this, and couldn't really see what the problem was. It was not as if Agios Nikolaos was party central. If they were tourists, they were likely to be the quiet, interested-in-history-and-culture types.

'For their representatives.'

Mia stared. Holiday reps? She had heard stories of course, who hadn't? Stories of endless parties, late nights and general wildness.

'But it was so quiet,' she said.

'It is flight day. They have been ferrying people to the airport and picking up the next batch. Once they have dropped them all off, they will be back.'

Mia took a sip of wine as she digested this piece of news. She had chosen a UK holiday let because she had assumed it would be easier to manage the booking and payment. She had not considered who might be living next door. She felt a hand on her arm and looked up into Alessandro's face which was the picture of concern.

'Do not worry, Mia. I'm sure you will get on with everyone fine.'

'I doubt it,' she said gloomily, having a flashback of life at her sixth form college. 'I'm not exactly the fun, partying type.'

'Now, that I don't believe,' he said, his eyes suddenly serious. Mia's heart dropped another notch. Why did all the lovely handsome guys feel the need to party hard and drink till they fell over? It was a mystery that she had yet to solve.

'Just not my thing. I'm more of a go out for a nice meal with friends kind of person.'

'Then you have come to the right place,' Elizabeth said, directing a mismatched collection of young and old to seats around the table.

'Nikolas family, meet Mia, a friend of Alex. Mia, meet the family.' She

22

proceeded to introduce everyone, but Mia quickly lost track and just returned each smile. Clearly she had misread all the signals. This was no romantic dinner for two. Instead, it was more like a family dinner back home, with everyone shouting over each other and handing round plates of food. She felt the disappointment simmer in her gut. She would need to give herself a good talking to later. Meeting a man, however lovely he was, was not part of the plan. However, it didn't mean that she couldn't let her hair down a little, enjoy the excellent food and watch the dynamics of another family, without the need to be a referee.

3

When Mia had failed to stifle another yawn, Alex stood up and held out his hand.

'Time for you to go home, I think. You must be tired after a day of travel.'

Mia took it gratefully, and stood to shouts from other members of Alex's family which she felt sure ran along the lines of 'it's too early to leave'. Alex said something in Greek and there was much nodding and agreement and Mia was waved off.

'What did you say?' Mia asked.

'I promised you would be back tomorrow night, feeling more refreshed.' Alex grinned at her. 'I hope you don't mind?' he added.

'Not at all, your family have made me very welcome.'

Mia smiled but inside her head there was an edge to the comment. Whilst she had thoroughly enjoyed the evening, she did not want to get drawn into the minute-by-minute life of a large family. She had one of those back home and it was one of the reasons she had come to Crete.

'You have to eat, yes?' he said, and Mia wondered if he could read her mind. 'Don't look so worried, we all have jobs and school, you will have much time to yourself, I think.'

Mia smiled a little guiltily. 'I don't mean to be ungrateful, it's just I came to Crete because I couldn't seem to make the time to write at home and I only have six months before I have to go back. I want to make the most of it.' Her words spilled out in a rush and she had a sudden surge of worry that she had insulted him and his family.

'You are writing a book?' Mia could see his eyes sparkle with interest and relaxed a little.

'Trying to,' she said, a little ruefully. They walked slowly through the streets and Mia took in the old buildings and balconies overflowing with bright flowers from window boxes.

'One thing you must learn about us,' Alex said, 'we are laid back here. We would enjoy your company whenever you feel able to join us.'

Mia wondered if the 'us' meant 'me' but forced the thought from her mind. She stopped and looked at him.

'I'm sorry, you must think I am very rude.'

'Not at all, your directness is refreshing. If only all of us could be so focused on achieving our goals.'

He started to walk again and Mia fell in beside him. As they turned a corner the noise of thumping music hit her and she stopped in her tracks. Alex had been right; her quiet, peaceful apartment had been turned into a nightclub. The pool, previously deserted, was now alive with people, some sat around the edges, and others jumping in, screaming. Everywhere were empty bottles and cans and someone had set up a raucous drinking game.

Since Mia did not want to appear boring or a party pooper in front of Alex, she said, 'Well, I'd best go and meet the neighbours. Thank you for dinner and for walking me home.'

Alex looked at her a little doubtfully and opened his mouth to comment but appeared to think better of it.

'Dinner is at eight every night, come join us if you would like.'

'Thank you,' she said, and then feeling daring, placed a quick kiss on his cheek. He smelled of warm weather and a hint of lemon which made her pause to drink it in.

'Good night,' she said, slightly breathlessly, and waved at his retreating back. She waited for a moment, willing it to happen, and then it did. He turned around, grinned and waved.

What Mia really needed now was some sleep and some time to process all that had happened to her — and maybe to dream a little of Alessandro, the handsome Greek. The apartment had two entrances, and Mia chose to walk around

27

the building to the front, not feeling brave enough to traverse the large groups of people by the pool. The door was stood wide open, despite the sign asking for it to remain closed at all times. Mia pulled it to behind her and headed for the stairs. At the bottom of the stairs a couple were kissing passionately and Mia had to squeeze past them. Lost in the moment, they ignored her.

As quickly as she could, she ran to her room and locked the door behind her. The air in her room was like the inside of a pressure cooker. She walked over to the balcony and pulled back the double glazed doors, only to be hit by a wave of noise. Wishing she had gone for a room with air conditioning, she closed it again and switched on the small fan that had been left in her room.

Mia showered in blissfully cold water and then put on her shorty pyjamas. She checked her tablet for messages from home, read them and then checked her schedule for Day One. Her day would start at 07.00, as it did at home. She had decided that since this was not technically a holiday, she should try and stay on a work-like timetable. She reached across for her travel alarm clock and set it for 6.50, giving herself her usual ten-minute snooze period.

★   ★   ★

The shrill alarm had Mia out of bed and assuming a ninja fighting stance. Her sleep-addled brain tried to process what it was. A yell from the apartment next door and banging on the adjoining wall told her that the noise was of her own making. She dived onto the bed, grabbed her alarm clock and muffled it with a pillow whilst trying to switch it off by feel alone. Beautiful silence returned and Mia breathed a sigh of relief which was quickly followed by a flash of anger. Her neighbours had not exactly been sensitive to her needs and yet she was supposed to tiptoe around them until their hangovers wore off! They had finally passed out around four-thirty. Between the music, screaming, and laughing she had been able to sleep in only fits and starts. Her first proper writing day and she felt like a slug who had wandered over some slug pellets by mistake, all dehydrated and shrivelled.

What she needed was a cup of tea and maybe some breakfast, containing lots of sugar to get her going. She forced herself to get out of bed, despite the fact that she was sure she could hear it calling to her. She was not going to give up on her plans so easily. She showered quickly and changed. With everything that happened last night, she had not bought milk and since she couldn't face black tea she had one choice: to go out and get some. She picked up her brightly coloured beach bag, checked for her purse and tablet and opened her door.

Outside her room was a trail of rubbish, glass bottles and cans. It was worse than living with students. Mia just knew this was not going to work, and she had to fight back the tears that threatened to ruin the first day of her big adventure.

Swiftly, she made up her mind. Turning back into her room, she grabbed her precious notebook and decided to head out in search of a place to write. It was clear that she would not get anything done here, especially once her neighbours roused themselves, but maybe she could find a café somewhere that would be peaceful and give her the space to think about where she could move to.

Out on the streets, all was quiet. The shutters of the older buildings remained firmly closed. She wandered back through the maze of small side streets but found nothing open — no shops or cafés, nothing. She felt lost. This was not how it was supposed to be. She felt the tears and a touch of loneliness well up inside her. A car drove past her with a sharp toot of the horn and it braked sharply. With the window down Mia could see the driver and she didn't think she had ever been more happy to see anyone.

'Good morning Mia,' Alex called. 'You are up early. I'm afraid in Crete we sleep in, so you will not find much open at this hour.'

'So it seems! To be honest, I was just after a shop to buy some milk and maybe somewhere quiet to sit.'

'The shop by the big hotel is open at nine but that's a bit of a wait. I'm heading back to the taverna and I could rustle you up some coffee?'

Mia was not a big coffee fan but right now that sounded like heaven.

'Do you mind?'

She was rewarded with the grin that made her stomach flutter.

'I am in need of a coffee myself and I have time before my next job'.

Alex got out of the car and they walked to the taverna together.

'Would I be right in guessing that the party went on all night?'

Mia, conscious that she must look pale and worn out, lifted a hand to her face.

'They all started to pass out around four-thirty, so I suppose I should consider myself lucky.'

Mia swallowed as the tears that had been close to the surface threatened to break through. The last thing she wanted to do was cry on Alessandro's shoulder.

'I'm sure it will get better though,' she said, with forced cheerfulness. Her fake smiled dropped when she saw Alex's face.

'I'm afraid that the reputation of the Ambrosia apartments would suggest otherwise.'

'You're probably right. I'll have to start looking for somewhere else.' Mia's stomach gave another lurch, and this time it had nothing to do with Alex's closeness. She had arrived at the start of the season and she suspected that everywhere would be booked up for months.

Alex pulled out a key and unlocked the front door to the taverna.

'Why don't we sit out here, if it is not too cool for you?'

'Here would be lovely.'

Mia watched as he disappeared inside, then dived into her bag and pulled out her tablet. If she needed a new place to live then she had better get started straight away. A few minutes later, Alex reappeared with a tray laden with yoghurt, fruit, bread and a jar of honey.

'I have a surprise for you, which I think you will like,' Alex said as he pulled out a small china teapot.

Mia could have kissed him, although if she was honest she had felt like that since the moment she met him.

'Ma cannot quite rid herself of the desire for a cup of tea. Her family sends it over from the UK. She says the imported stuff doesn't taste the same.'

'Thank you,' Mia said, pouring herself a cup and adding a dash of milk. It was amazing, she thought as she took a sip, how a cup of tea could make everything better. Alex laughed.

'You look just like my ma when she has her first cup in the morning, she drinks it like it is the nectar of the gods.'

'You don't like it?' she asked. Alex shook his head and lifted up his mug of black coffee.

'No, I take after my father in this regard. Please help yourself.' He gestured to the food.

Mia had thought that after all she

had eaten last night she would not need breakfast, but the smell of warm bread was too much for her and she copied Alex, slathering it first in butter and then honey. Never had something so simple tasted so good!

A drizzle of honey ran down her chin and Alex reached over and wiped it away with his thumb. Mia blinked at such an intimate gesture, but Alex looked nonchalant as if this was also common practice in Greece. Mia took a deep breath and tried to force her heart from a gallop to a trot.

'So, I think we need to solve your accommodation problem,' Alex said out loud as Mia watched a local woman open the shutters to her apartment and let in the warm, sweet-smelling air.

'Not going to be easy,' Mia said, although it seemed to bother her less now she had a cup of tea and a full stomach.

'I hope you don't mind, but I spoke to my uncle last night. He owns several houses which are now small apartments. He has one that would be available if you would like it? It's small but I think you will find it more to your liking.'

Mia took a moment to digest this information. Could she have found an answer so easily? She couldn't overlook that Alex had ridden to her rescue yet again, and she felt extremely grateful.

'I can take you to see it, if you aren't sure?'

Mia laughed; clearly her silence had made him think that she didn't want it, when nothing could have been further from the truth.

'I don't need to see it first, thank you. Anything would be better than where I am currently living.'

'That's settled then. Uncle Vasili gave me the keys, so we can move you in later if you like? I have work but I could be free around seven?'

'Perfect.'

Mia heaved a sigh of relief. It would give her time to contact the holiday company, make her feelings clear and demand her money back!

4

Despite the bad start to the day, Mia had managed to hit her word count and she couldn't help feeling pleased with herself. Alex had suggested a friend's café where she might write in peace, and which also had free Wi-Fi. He had walked her to the café and, it appeared to Mia, left with great reluctance to take a business man to the airport. For the first time in her life she had lost track of time and lost herself in her writing, in a way that she had never managed at home with the endless interruptions. When she arrived at the front of the dreaded apartment, she found Alex waiting for her leaning against his taxi.

'Sorry I'm late,' she said, feeling guilty. She hated being late. Alex shrugged.

'You aren't. I'm early, the traffic was better than expected.'

'I just need to shove a few things back

into my suitcase and I should be ready.'

This wasn't exactly true, as Mia had completely unpacked the belongings that would see her through the next six months, in the mistaken belief that this would be her home.

'I'll come and help,' he said, stepping forward and holding the door open for her, ever the gentleman.

Mia didn't have the heart to tell him she would prefer to pack up by herself. The stairwell and pool area seemed to have been transformed back to their previous orderly state and there was no evidence that a rave had happened just the evening before. She unlocked the door and let Alex in to the room, before opening the glass doors to let some air in. Alex stepped out on to the balcony as Mia pulled out her suitcase and started to pile her clothes back into it. Normally she would take time to do this but, with Alex waiting, she didn't want to appear too fastidious. She had just emptied her underwear drawer when Alex spoke.

'Nice plan,' he said, and Mia froze.

In amongst it all, she had forgotten that she had stuck up her six-month plan and her longer-term plan on the wall of her room. She felt herself blush. She had never shared this with anyone and now here was this gorgeous man, that she couldn't seem to help fancying, having a good old look at it. She tried to cross the room casually but knew that she looked anything but. Hurriedly, she pulled it off the wall and it crumpled into a heap on the floor.

'Here, let me,' Alex said, picking it up and carefully rolling it. 'You are a great planner, I see.'

Mia glanced at him, checking to see if he was teasing like her family back home. Seeing no malice, she shrugged.

'I just don't think you can expect what you want to simply fall into your lap. You have to work at it, and you need to plan — well, plan the bits you can.' She added the afterthought, remembering how her ten year plan from twenty to thirty had so far failed miserably on one point. She had not met the man of her dreams, been swept off her feet and married in the eight years since she had turned twenty. Since the plans she had for the following decades had been based solely on this assumption, she'd had to rip them up, and in the process she had started to wonder if relying on planning was really the way forward.

Alex handed her the rolled up sheet and she could feel him watching her closely.

'A very English philosophy,' he said. 'In Crete, we are much more about sitting back and waiting to see what happens.' His eyes seemed alive and Mia felt caught in his gaze.

'And how does that work for you?' Mia said softly, aware that the distance between them was now very small.

'Well,' he said, reaching out and holding her hand, 'I could wait until you ask me to kiss you or I could follow your philosophy.'

'Which would be … ?' Mia managed to say, despite her heart leaping all around inside her chest.

'If I were to follow your approach,' he

40

said, lifting his hand to smooth back the hair that had escaped her sloppy bun, 'I would have planned to get you all by yourself, somewhere beautiful and romantic ... ' They were so close now that there was no longer any gap between them, and Mia felt as if their hearts were beating in unison. 'Then as the sun set I would reach for you, take you in my arms and kiss you.' Suddenly not wanting to wait for the sunset, despite how delicious it sounded, she stood on her tiptoes and gently brushed her lips against his. He smiled now.

'Perhaps the Greek way is best,' he whispered, before pulling her into his arms and kissing her until her head spun.

Mia felt like time had stood still and she also felt as if she had never been kissed before. She had certainly never been kissed before like this. It felt like she had found the other half that would make her whole.

Alex gently drew away and she had to fight the urge to hold him tight.

'Forgive me, I could not help myself. I

would not want you to think I was taking advantage of you.'

Mia smiled reassuringly.

'I'm pretty sure I started it,' she said with a giggle, realising that she had never been the one to make the first move in a relationship, ever. She was rewarded with a warm smile that made her insides melt and her legs turn to jelly.

'We should get on, or you will have to stay here another night,' he said, and the thought of another sleepless night, listening to all the sounds that went with partying, was just about enough to make her sigh, step back and return to her shoddy packing.

*   *   *

Alex drove through the narrow back streets of Agios Nikolaos. Mia did not need to be told that this was the real heart of the town, where the locals lived, away from the tourist traps. The old buildings leaned across the street as if they were trying to touch each other and lines of laundry hung in the warm evening air. Alex pulled up outside a three-storey house which had a battered blue wooden front door. As Mia stepped out of the taxi she could smell flowers and hear the sounds of the evening meal being prepared. Alex hauled her suitcase out of the boot of the taxi and Mia offered to take it.

'There are no lifts in this building, Mia. I think you would struggle to carry all of your belongings up the stairs.'

He wheeled the suitcase up to the front door and pulled a tarnished silver key attached to a link of worry beads from his pocket.

Mia blinked as her eyes adjusted to the gloom. They were in a small hallway with a door to the right of them and a narrow staircase to the left. She watched Alex easily lift her heavy suitcase up two flights of stairs, following close behind so she had the best opportunity to admire him, without him knowing. On the third floor he opened the only door and gestured that Mia should step inside.

'Welcome home,' he said, and Mia

could see that he was studying her closely to gauge her reaction.

The apartment was essentially one room, with a small alcove that housed the shower and toilet. There was a floor length glass door to the rear of the room which opened out on to a tiny balcony. Mia caught her breath as she took in the view. Over rows and rows of red and white tiled roofs she could see the sea and the sun falling behind the horizon. There was a double bed, an old two-seater sofa, and a small table in the kitchenette area, which had a table-top stove and an ancient fridge.

'It's a little basic perhaps, in comparison with the newer apartments, but it is very Greek.'

Mia couldn't help smiling at the concern in his voice. He was obviously worried that she didn't like it.

'Alex, it's perfect. Thank you!'

He crossed the room to stand beside her as she turned her attention to the view.

'I hope it will not be a distraction,' he said, indicating the view. Mia shook her head.

'More like inspiration.'

She leaned across and kissed him on the cheek. He turned his body and pulled her into his arms and kissed her, his hands gently cradling her face. Mia felt lost in the moment, but this time it was her that drew back.

'We'll be late for supper,' she whispered, drinking in every angle of his face.

'You are coming?' He seemed surprised.

'Of course. You said yesterday that I would come back ... ' She felt a twinge of uncertainty — did he not want her to come?

'I did. I was just trying to make it easier for you if you did not want to! You are always welcome, but I will understand if you want to write.'

She kissed him again. To be both gorgeous and so understanding seemed nothing short of miraculous!

'Don't need to, I've hit my target for the day.'

It was great to be able to share this

with someone who would appreciate the achievement. Back home, nobody seemed to have the time to be interested, always rushing off to do the next thing.

'Congratulations,' he said seriously, and he looked impressed, which sent a shiver of excitement down her spine. This man really was perfect! 'In that case, let us go. I have something else to show you.'

5

Mia was sat at the beautiful old, well-worn, olive wood desk that Alex said he had found for her at a shop that sold second-hand furniture. She had tried to pay for it, but he had refused, saying it was a gift and then he proceeded to give her a very gentle lecture that to refuse a gift in Greece could be considered insulting. She had then gone into full apology mode, which only made him laugh. They had tried it in various places around her one-room apartment but had settled on the window that overlooked the narrow street. Alex had been right — the view of the sea seemed able to suck hours of time into its vortex. The street provided interest and the odd distraction but she was still able to pound out her daily word count.

Mia picked up her mobile and checked again for messages. If Alex had no fares to drive at lunchtime then he would send her a message to ask if she was at a good place to stop, and if she was, they would have lunch together. Sometimes they would eat out — Mia insisted that they took turns in paying — and sometimes he would bring lunch and they would go down to the sea and eat. Far from being a distraction from her writing, Mia found she focused more, knowing that she did not want to miss the opportunity to see Alex. If she even so much as hinted that she was behind then he would refuse to take her out, instead dropping her off some fresh bread and then taking his leave.

Her phone remained resolutely blank and so she turned her attention back to her notebook, spread out on the desk before her, and picked up her favourite pen, an old ink one that had been her grandmother's. There was something about writing by hand that made Mia feel more connected with the words she was writing. She had never been persuaded that typing her writing, while arguably quicker, was better.

Pushing thoughts and images of Alex from her mind, she focused on her story. She had a detailed plan — of course! — and character sketches, but what she had come up with at home seemed now a little flat and lifeless, and with every page she wrote she changed both character and story.

The beep from her phone made her jump. Forcing herself to finish writing the sentence first, she picked up the phone and texted back a smiley face which was their shorthand for 'Yes please!'

Ten minutes later and Mia had changed into a floral peasant top and long skirt, found her flip-flops and brushed out her hair. A swipe of lip gloss and she was heading down the stairs to wait for Alex in the shadow of the building. She loved to be there before him, as it afforded her the opportunity to watch him stride down the road and see the expression on his face when he first caught sight of her. The sight of him made her heart sing. Elizabeth had been right, the island and its men, specifically Alex, had a magical quality and she knew she was under its spell.

'Yasou, Mia.'

'Yasou,' Mia replied, just starting to feel less self-conscious about her poor accent.

Alex kissed her gently and she returned in kind.

'I thought perhaps we would have lunch by the port. I am told they have a fine catch of fish today and it will be cooler by the sea.'

Mia's stomach answered the question with a loud rumble and they both laughed. Alex held out his hand and Mia took it, feeling that wonderful sense of belonging to someone, and they wound their way through the streets to the port.

Whilst they waited for their fish to be cooked, Alex made his usual enquiries about her writing and her progress. Mia answered them but had been determined today that she would find out more about him. He talked little of himself, claiming that he was not interesting and when pushed would regale her with tales of his extended family both ancient and modern. But today would be different.

Mia cleared her throat. She had rehearsed this in her head, but now she was sat opposite him she felt suddenly shy.

'So, enough of me. I want to know more about you.' Previously, she had stopped here and judged his reaction, but today she didn't want to be put off. 'What did you study in London?' she asked, figuring this was fairly neutral ground. She watched as he took a sip of iced water.

'It does not matter. I never finished.'

'If you were prepared to leave all this and travel to England I imagine it must have been important to you once?'

He nodded in acknowledgement.

'But it cannot be and to dwell on it does nothing.' He looked away from her now and gazed out to sea. Mia waited in silence to see if he would offer an explanation but none came.

'Why did you come home?'

'I missed my family.'

Mia gave a guilty smile. She did miss her family, but not enough to go home early.

'And, with the economy as it was, I was needed back here.' He turned to look at her now, and for the first time she saw pain in his eyes.

'The taverna is successful, but in these times it is not enough. My parents hid the truth from me for a year, but I knew that something was wrong. Ma was quiet, not her usual self and I knew. So I didn't tell them. I just flew home and got a job driving the taxi. Between us we make enough to pay the bills and keep the taverna open.'

Mia reached across the table and squeezed his hand.

'I'm sorry, Alex.'

'Do not be sorry.' His voice had a sudden harsh quality to it and she withdrew a little.

'Forgive me,' he said, softening. 'What I mean is that nothing is more important than my family. There will be time later for dreams, I am sure.' He took a deep breath and his smile was back. 'But you understand if I do not wish to speak of it.'

'Of course,' Mia said out loud, but in her head she wondered if there was anything she could do to help Alex realise his dreams, as he was helping her.

★   ★   ★

If Mia had any hope of being able to help Alex, she needed to find out some facts, and she felt sure that a few questions to the right people would provide all she needed.

Alex had asked if she wanted to join the family for dinner and she had agreed. She arrived at the taverna early and, as had become her habit, she helped Elizabeth to set up the table and lay out cutlery and glasses. She had never been able to persuade them to take any money for feeding her and so, after the first few times, she had spoken to Elizabeth and insisted that she doing something for her in return. Now that Alex had told her what had been going on with the family's finances, she was even more glad that she had done so.

'All done,' Mia said, placing the remaining forks and knives onto the bar which Elizabeth was wiping down. 'What can I do next?'

'You can sit and talk with me. Tell me how your writing is going.'

'Really well,' Mia said. 'When I was at home, I dreamt of what it would be like to have the time to write, but I never imagined that it would be quite as wonderful as this. You were right about the magic of the island.'

Elizabeth smiled. 'And about the magic of its men?'

Mia laughed. Before she had arrived, she would have been embarrassed to talk of such things, especially to her boyfriend's mother, but Elizabeth felt like family.

'That too.'

'I am glad. I have not seen Alex this happy for some time. No mother likes to see their child so lost.' Elizabeth's face was crumpled with a frown.

'Lost, how?' asked Mia.

'I think that it is for Alex to tell you, if he wants to.'

Mia nodded.

'I asked him today about what he studied in the UK.'

Elizabeth stopped wiping the bar top.

'And what did he say?'

'He didn't want to talk about it. He just said that he came home.' Mia chose her words carefully, as the last thing she wanted to do was to cause upset. She knew that Elizabeth would not have wanted Alex to give up on his dream.

'He won't talk of it with me either,' she said sadly. 'I try to persuade him that we can manage and that he can go back, but he says he doesn't want to, that he wants to be at home. I don't believe him.'

'He loves being here, Elizabeth. Perhaps he was just homesick?' Mia suddenly needed to make her friend feel better.

'There is a time for family and a time to follow what your heart wants. You know that, as do I. That is what I want for Alessandro, but he is stubborn, just like his father.'

She smiled now and Mia could feel the mood lighten a little.

'And then there is you, and I thank God for you. He is more like my old Alex with you here.'

Mia couldn't hide her grin.

'He has changed my life too. I've never met anyone like him.'

The last sentence spilled out and she raised a hand to cover her mouth as if she was afraid she would say more. Elizabeth picked up her hand and kissed it.

'Alessandro!' she said looking up. 'We have been waiting for you. Come, come,' she said, going in to full matriarchal mode. As she turned away from Mia, she gave her a quick warning glance and Mia nodded. She understood. Alex was not to know what they had been speaking about. But Mia knew she would not be able to let it go. She had to do something to help all of them, all she needed to do was work out what that something was.

6

After a loud and late supper Alex walked Mia home.

'I think I can guess what you studied,' she said, in what she hoped was a teasing voice. He raised an eyebrow but didn't look particularly cross. 'I looked at the University website and when I saw it I knew.' They continued to walk hand in hand and Mia knew she had his attention.

'And?' he asked when she said nothing.

'Space Science,' she said, holding her breath a little and praying he would laugh. She was rewarded. His peal of laughter seemed to reverberate around the buildings.

'You think I want to be a space man?' he said once his laughter had died down.

Mia shrugged.

'I could see you in one of those big suits with the helmet.' She mimed putting on a big helmet and then pretended to spacewalk. He laughed some more and she was glad that he did not seem to be upset.

'Why is it so important to you, I wonder?' he said, grabbing her hand to prevent her from moonwalking any further away.

'Because I care about you,' she said simply. 'You care about my dreams and I want to know what yours are.'

'Even if they can never be?' he asked softly.

'I don't believe that,' she said firmly.

'Not everyone gets to do what they want when they want, Mia.'

Mia suddenly felt as if she was being told off, like a school girl.

'What's that supposed to mean?' she said, trying to keep the crossness from her voice.

'You have left your family behind, yes?'

'I haven't exactly abandoned them!'

'Have you asked them how they feel about you being so far away?'

He seemed to know exactly what to say to get to that deep, nagging fear that she kept pushed well down.

'No, but not everything is about them. I'm sure they'll cope. It's only for six months.'

An unwanted image of her family appeared in her mind's eye, along with all the things that she had been doing for them, like picking up her niece from school.

'I was not so sure, and so I came home. I do not regret my decision.'

It was a statement, but it felt like an accusation.

'Neither do I,' Mia said.

Alex's face was passive but he was looking at her in that way which said he knew what she was thinking. Up till now she had enjoyed the sensation, but this time she just wanted to get away.

'You don't understand,' she said. 'I haven't told you everything.'

'And neither have I.'

'Well maybe you should!'

'Perhaps, but not tonight I think. Goodnight, Mia.'

He leaned across, pecked her on the cheek and strode away.

★   ★   ★

Mia was awake at dawn, wrapped in misery and feeling very sorry for herself. She could not believe that the dream had ended so quickly and so abruptly. She felt as if her bubble of happiness had been burst. Mia also knew that she had an acute case of feeling sorry for herself and that the reality of the situation probably bore little resemblance to the dramatic notions of her sleep-addled brain. What she needed to do was get up, have a cup of tea and get writing. It was hard to wallow when you had something purposeful to do. Then she could distract herself as she waited for Alex to text, which she told herself firmly he would. He had probably not given their conversation of the night before another thought, he was so laid back.

Somehow that thought was comforting, and Mia fell asleep again only to be woken by the shrill ringing of the alarm clock that had been especially chosen to get her out of bed and awake, no matter what the circumstances. She rolled over with a groan and slapped at the space on her bedside table where the noise was coming from. She was rewarded with a loud clanging noise and a clatter that told her in no uncertain terms she had broken her reliable timepiece. She let out another groan but this one was of frustration. Now she would have to go in search of a new one. Just as she was about to lower herself back in to her bath of self-pity, a ping told her that she had received a text. She leapt out of bed and quickly crossed to the kitchenette, which had the only free plug in her tiny apartment.

Impatiently she waited for the message to appear on the screen, hoping that Alex would have returned to his usual easy manner.

'Tash missing. Text if she is with you.'

The message was from her older sister, Sally. Mia frowned and tried to work out what on earth was going on. Natasha was her little sister, twenty-four years old and, like the rest of her family, not exactly what you would call reliable. Her dad always described Tasha as loveably ditzy, having managed to get herself and the test examiner lost on her fourth, unsuccessful driving test. Tash rarely appeared where she was supposed to be on the right day, let alone at the right time, and relied on her besotted fiancé, Tim, to basically survive day to day life. As Mia's weariness faded it was replaced with a sharp tang of worry.

As the thought raised its ugly head that she had known, deep down, that something bad would happen if she wasn't around, Mia had to reach for the chair at her desk and sit down. She forced a deep breath into her lungs and mentally pushed the panic away. There was bound to be a simple and logical explanation, but Sally was good at neither of these.

'Have you checked with Tim?'

Mia almost felt silly for asking the question, but in situations with panicked family members it was always worth starting with the blindingly obvious. She waited, drumming her fingers on the desk and wondering if she should just call and damn the expense. A ping told her Sally had replied.

'They split up.'

Mia blinked and made herself read the text several times. Her brain tried to work out if predictive texting could be interfering with Sally's intended message, but whichever way she looked at it she could not work out what the message might mean.

'Tim hasn't seen her since. Mum frantic.' Another ping and another message.

This was all the news that Mia needed to ignore the expense and ring home. Her little sister really was missing. She didn't know which was more shocking, the fact that Tim and Tasha had split, or the fact that in a moment of crisis Tasha had taken herself off somewhere.

Mia hung up after she'd spoken to a tearful Sally, and tried to work out what to do next. She had been dreading a moment like this. A moment that could not be planned or prepared for. She had suspected that her family would have some crisis or other and ask her to come back to sort it out, to be the calming influence or the peacemaker, as seemed to be her designated role. But not for a moment had she thought it would be something like this. Tasha was gone, there was no trace of her. She had not spoken to a soul since she had had a terrific blow-up with Tim. Arguing was not like either of them; they had been in love ever since Tim had rescued Tasha from an older boy's teasing at primary school. She had taken no clothes with her and left her mobile at the flat she shared with Tim. No one had realised she was missing until Tim had turned up at her parents' house in the morning to return it. When realisation dawned on them, her parents had called the police but been told there was nothing they could do until Tasha had been missing for forty-eight hours.

Mia had spent some time trying to reassure both her mum and sister, who tearfully blamed themselves, Tim and anyone else. The only name not spoken in the list was her own, but Mia knew that it was there nonetheless. Her mum was convinced that Tasha was currently making her way to Mia in Crete. Mia herself thought it was more likely Tasha was holed up in the Hotel Express in town, and said as much. She hung up with the agreement that her dad would check there and that Mia herself would travel to the nearest airport in Crete and check all the new arrivals.

Since Tasha had never travelled further than school on her own Mia couldn't see her leaving the country, but despite all her reassurances to her family, she was worried and knew that the activity might at least give her a sense of purpose. As if the memory of the night before had been wiped from her mind, she picked up the phone and dialled Alex's number. A first, since they normally communicated by text.

'Hello Mia.'

His voice made tears spring to her eyes and she wiped them away with an angry palm; she didn't have the time or the luxury to fall apart.

'Alex …' Her throat closed up and she couldn't find any words to speak.

'Mia?' His voice was full of concern and it made Mia's heart leap despite everything.

'I need you,' she whispered.

'I'll be right there.'

As she rung off she contemplated the words. There had been no hesitation or doubt in his voice, and she wondered if he had completely forgotten the events of the night before. Mia was immediately ashamed of her moment of self-absorption. None of that mattered right now. All that mattered was finding Tasha.

7

Mia sat beside Alex as they raced towards the airport. They had exchanged few words; Mia had told him what had happened and Alex had simply led her to his car.

'We should be there in time for the first flight from Gatwick. Do you think she would fly from there?' Alex's voice startled Mia from her fretting.

'Before today I would have said there was no chance of Tasha even travelling to the airport on her own, let alone getting on a plane, but she has to be somewhere.' Mia involuntarily offered up a prayer. 'Oh, please just let her be safe.'

'I'm sure Tasha can look after herself,' Alex said glancing from the road. 'She will be fine.'

His words somehow reminded Mia of their angry exchange the night before. Was he just saying that to make her feel better? Did he believe it, or did he believe that this was all her fault, for abandoning her family? Mia glanced at him now and took in his look of concentration as he navigated through the traffic and people safely. She wondered if it would make her feel better to have someone speak out loud the words that her family had not said: that if she had stayed at home, put her family first, none of this would have happened.

'It's my fault.' The words flew from her mouth before she realised she had said them. The tears she had kept at bay now sprang forth and she turned her head to look sightlessly out of the window.

'No, Mia, how could it possibly be your fault?' Mia felt his hand reach for hers, his touch familiar and comforting. 'You do not yet know what has happened. Perhaps Tasha is just taking some time to think about things.'

'You don't know Tasha,' Mia said with a sniff. 'She won't go on the Tube on her own. She likes to be at home, with people she knows. Adventure is so not her thing.'

'But I know you, Mia, and I think your sister is not so different.' Alex took his eyes off of the road briefly and looked at her. 'You have surprised yourself, no? Since being here. You have embraced the Greek way of life, even managing on occasion to be a little late.'

He squeezed her hand again and Mia managed a watery smile. He was right of course, she had always been driven by order and planning and whilst that was still a part of her life she had also managed to release her grip a little and relax.

'There is more to your sister also, I think. She will always be the baby to you but like steel you cannot know how strong it is until it is tested.'

★   ★   ★

Alex's words echoed in her ears as she paced the shiny floor of the arrivals lounge. There was nothing to do now but wait. She had no flight details and no idea if Tasha was even on a plane. With one eye on the large clock she forced herself to wait a whole minute between checks of her mobile. She knew it was pointless anyway, since it would ping if a message arrived, but somehow she needed to do something.

Alex returned and handed her a paper cup. Mechanically, Mia took a sip and then grimaced.

'Sorry, no tea,' Alex said.

'It's fine, thank you. I don't think even tea would help right now.'

'A flight from Southampton has just landed. Do you think she would travel from there?'

Mia shook her head.

'I doubt it. It would be much easier for her to get to Gatwick or Heathrow.'

Even as she said it, she thought through every one of Tasha's friends for a connection to Southampton, but found none.

A few people appeared through the gates, those without luggage in the hold. Since Tasha had left home with nothing, she would not need to wait for the suitcase carousel. Mia scanned the faces, cursing the surge of hope she felt before she realised that Tasha was not among them. She could feel her shoulders sag and she felt overwhelmed by a sense of fear and uncertainty. A warm hand reached for hers and gave her the strength to stay on her feet. When her phone made the familiar pinging noise, her hand shook as she tried to press the button to open the message.

'Here, let me.' Alex's voice was quiet but insistent and Mia released her grip. 'It is from Sally. She says there is no sign of Tasha at any of the local hotels.'

She had known as much, feeling sure if they had found her they would have called. She could feel his eyes on her face. She nodded, not knowing what to say to him in that moment. The arrivals area was starting to fill up and the noise levels were now at cheerfully loud. Holiday reps had appeared and were shepherding new holiday makers to the right coaches and dealing with the inevitable questions and complaints.

'Mia,' Alex said, with an edge of excitement to his voice, 'is that Tasha?'

Mia was not sure she could bear to look and be disappointed. She forced herself to follow his pointed finger, but all she could see was a small child having a meltdown and parents trying to corral the rest of their brood. Mia moved to one side and tried to see what Alex had seen but the family seemed to move as one, like a solid wall had suddenly sprung up. Mia moved the other way and they followed as if they were mirroring her every move. She ran an angry hand through her hair and hissed in frustration. Alex grabbed her hand again and steered her around them. People were milling around now and if Alex hadn't pointed the figure out Mia was sure she would have missed her.

She almost looked too young to be Tasha, sat on a low wall with head down. She had no bags with her except a small purse worn across her chest. Mia couldn't be sure who it was but before she knew it she was running and Alex was keeping pace.

'Tasha!' someone yelled and it took Mia a few steps to realise it was her. The figure didn't move or react and Mia's heart clenched in her chest at the thought that it wasn't her — but that wasn't enough to stop her running. A few more steps and she was there, standing before the small figure.

'Tasha?' Mia said softly. 'Tasha, honey, it's Mia.'

The tear-streaked face that turned to her could not have looked more beautiful to Mia, and a heartbeat later she held her sobbing baby sister in her arms.

★　★　★

Mia felt like she was sat in a vigil. Tasha was curled up in a tight ball, finally asleep. Mia reached over to stroke her hair for the millionth time, as if she was afraid she would vanish again at any minute. After a long phone call home, in which Mia had done her best to reassure her family that Tasha was safe — although not yet able to explain what had happened — and promised them that she would update them as soon as she could, they had left the airport. Tasha had been in such a state that Alex had carried her to his car and carefully placed her into the seat. The journey to her apartment had been long and Tasha had continued to cry whilst Mia kissed her head and held her tight.

Alex had delivered them both safely home and promised to return if Mia needed anything, then the two sisters had been left alone. Tasha did not seem to be able to talk, or maybe did not want to, so Mia had fed her some tea and then put her to bed, holding Tasha's hand tightly and promising that she would be there when she woke. Mia was just fighting off another frightening thought of what might have happened to Tasha, when there was a soft tap at the door. She could not help but smile when she saw Alex standing there with a look of warmth that made her toes tingle. Alex smiled and handed her a brown paper bag.

'Ma thought you might not want to come to the taverna tonight, although you are both welcome of course, so I brought you supper.'

Mia took a step back from the door to allow him to pass into the room.

'Are you sure that your sister is up for visitors?' he asked, and Mia was warmed by his sensitivity.

'Tasha is fast asleep and to be honest I could do with some company.'

Alex studied her face for a moment before nodding and stepping inside. He took in the small figure wrapped tightly in the bed.

'How is she?' His voice was soft and low.

'To be honest, I'm not sure. I've still no idea what has happened, but she seems to be in one piece, physically at least.'

Mia carefully lifted two plates from her small selection and set them down on the small table. The light was starting to fade and she reached for the candle in its holder. Alex pulled his lighter from his pocket and the candle sprang into life. They took their seats and Mia began to eat, her stomach emitting a loud noise which suggested that she was more hungry than she had thought. Alex laughed quietly.

'Ma was right, as always.'

'Please thank her for me, her food is so delicious I suspect that I may even be able to tempt Tasha when she wakes.'

Mia took a mouthful, savouring the sweet rice and pepper, then she put down her fork.

'Thank you, too. I know that you missed out on fares, but I don't know what I would have done without you today.'

Alex shrugged. 'We are friends, Mia. That is what friends do. It is a sad day when money is more important than that.'

Mia knew that Alex had not intended it but somehow the statement stung. Perhaps this was his way of saying that their argument had meant something and that he now only wanted to be friends? She swallowed the lump that had suddenly formed in her throat. She knew that she wanted more, plan or no plan. Alex was very special and she was sure she was falling in love — but perhaps it was destined to be another failed holiday romance. Away from home and the pressures of daily life, it was easy to be your best self. Perhaps the other night had given Alex a glimpse of who she really was, the person who had abandoned her family due to a selfish desire to follow her dreams.

Mia had forced herself to ignore the part of her that nagged with guilt that something bad might happen if she was away. She had made up her mind that her family would be fine, that they would cope, and now her worst, deepest fears had been realised. They had not been fine and something bad had happened, so bad that her baby sister, who had never travelled further than the end of the road by herself, had put herself on a plane to another country to find her. Everything had changed now and Tasha would be her priority and the focus of all her energy. If Alex wanted to be friends then she would accept that and be happy, even if her heart felt heavy at the thought.

8

Tasha slept for eleven hours straight, while Mia catnapped in the chair that she had pulled up by the double bed. Whilst she longed to find out what had happened, if only to stop her imagination coming up with more and more horrific events, Mia knew that what was best for Tash was to let her sleep. Stretching out all the cricks from sleeping upright in a chair, Mia moved quietly across the apartment and put the kettle on.

A rustling from the bed pulled her attention back to Tasha.

'Mia?' The voice sounded so young and afraid that Mia felt her heart tighten in her chest.

'I'm here, Tash. I'm right here.' With a few swift steps she was sat on the edge of the bed and she pulled her sister into her arms.

When Tasha's sobs had subsided, Mia

felt her pull away and she let her sit back in the bed.

'Tash, honey, can you tell me what happened?' Mia said softly. She watched as Tash gulped and worked hard to fight back another wave of tears.

'Tim and I … We … ' was all she could manage.

'I know sweetheart, Sally told me. Can you tell me what happened?'

Tasha shook her head fiercely like a child.

'I don't even know,' she half wailed. 'Everything was fine, the plans for the wedding and all of that, and then I just kind of wondered if there was more.'

'More what?' Mia asked, not entirely sure that she was following the conversation.

'More to life, I guess. I love Tim, I do, but I just wasn't sure that I didn't want to do more, see more.'

Mia couldn't hide her surprise, Tasha the ultimate home bird, wanting to see more? It just didn't seem possible.

'I told him that and he looked at me

just like you are now. He just didn't understand, no one understands.' Tasha shuddered with another sob and Mia reached out and squeezed her hand.

'I do understand, really I do. I'm just surprised, that's all.'

'Why? Because I've always done what everyone expected? Everyone treats me like the baby, like I can't do anything by myself, like I don't want to be more than that.'

'I'm sorry,' Mia said, and she meant it.

For all of her years she had thought that she was the only one trapped by what other people thought she should do, not able to dream for herself or step outside the role that they had given her to play.

'I never meant to make you feel that way, and I do know how that feels,' Mia said.

Tasha looked at her and her look was reproachful.

'But you did what you wanted.'

The nagging guilt was back and Mia tried to push it away without success.

'You just did it, you decided you

wanted to leave and so you did.'

'It wasn't quite like that. For starters, I told people where I was going.' Mia tried to inject a little humour but it became quickly apparent that Tasha was not ready for it.

'I would have told them, but they would have talked me out of it, then I would have stayed and been miserable, been trapped.'

'But what about Tim? He loves you.'

Tasha's lip wobbled. 'I love him too, but what if that's because he is the only one I've ever considered loving? What if there is someone else, something more?'

Mia raised an eyebrow. This was much more serious than a simple argument.

'I tried to explain it to him but he just looked so hurt and confused. I couldn't stand it, I couldn't take the words back and so ... I left and I came here, because I thought you would understand.'

Mia could see the pleading in her eyes. Tasha was so desperate for someone to understand and Mia knew how that felt. She thought that Alex was the first person to really understand her, and although their argument the night before might have changed their relationship, she also knew how good it was to feel that way.

'Of course I understand, Tasha, but I think perhaps you need to at least talk to Mum and Dad, tell them how you've been feeling. They've been really worried, you know.'

Tasha sniffed. 'I know, but I am twenty-four. I'm perfectly capable of looking after myself. They do fuss so.'

Mia smiled to herself as Tasha slid her feet out of bed and padded towards the bathroom, the image of the little girl, frightened and alone at the airport, fresh in her mind.

★   ★   ★

Tasha stepped out, freshly showered and dressed in a flowery, long summer dress of Mia's.

'So are you going to show me around?' Tasha asked.

Mia forced a smile. Her plan had been to

write today, but of course Tasha was more important. She wanted to ask Tash what her plans were, but knew it was too soon.

'Yep, but first ... ' Mia handed her the phone. 'Mum and Dad, Sally and then Tim.'

Mia watched Tasha's face drop.

'Tim?' she asked, again reminding Mia of a little girl.

'Tim,' Mia said firmly. 'He's been out of his mind with worry, the least you can do is reassure him that you're ok. Maybe tell him you just need a bit of time and space or something. You don't need to be making any big decisions right now.'

With the face of a sulky teenager, Tasha snatched the phone and stomped off to the back of the apartment where she could make her phone calls in relative privacy. Mia sighed. Somehow, her life in Crete had just turned into an episode of her life back home.

★   ★   ★

As they approached the taverna, Mia wondered at the amount of tourist-y stuff

83

they had managed to fit into one short day. Tasha had wanted to see everything, and that included all the tacky, made-for-English-tourists things. They had even had lunch in the English Bulldog pub which, Tasha had squealed in excitement was 'like home away from home.' Not for the first time Mia had marvelled that two sisters could be so fundamentally different. But now it was Mia's turn. She was determined to show Tasha what 'real' Crete was like and so she was taking her to family dinner.

They arrived at the taverna, early as usual, or at least early by Greek standards. The restaurant was empty and dark and Mia noticed that Tasha had not walked on to the veranda with her as if she was afraid that it was closed and they were trespassing. With a smile, Mia held out her hand and Tasha took it, allowing herself to be pulled into the dim light.

'Elizabeth?' Mia called, and was rewarded with a cry of surprise from the back room, which housed the kitchen.

'Mia! We did not expect to see you!' Elizabeth rushed forward and kissed Mia on each cheek before pulling her into a tight hug.

'And this must be Natasha,' Elizabeth said with a warm smile, before she hugged Tasha as if she were her own daughter who had been lost. Mia watched as Tasha, tense at first, melted into the hug, and she suspected that Tasha was reminded of home and their own mum.

'Welcome, little one. As I told our Mia on her first visit, this is your home too and we are your family. Now what can I get you to drink?'

'White wine, please,' Tasha said, and smiled. Mia could see that a lot of Tash's shyness had melted away, and she was grateful that Elizabeth had not mentioned the panic of the day before or anything about the reason that Tasha was here, instead treating her as if she were on holiday. Mia did not think that Tasha was quite ready to share with strangers, however friendly they might be.

'Now I see why you are so happy here,'

Tasha whispered as they made their way to the long table at the back of the taverna that served as the family dinner table. 'You've found yourself another family.' Mia studied her carefully, wondering if she was being spiteful but Tasha's smile said differently.

'They are lovely and very welcoming, but don't think I don't miss you all,' Mia said, feeling that to say anything else would be disloyal.

'Of course you do,' said Tasha firmly, 'but missing family doesn't mean that you have to be miserable and that you can't find happiness and adventure away from them.'

Mia smiled and lifted her glass to chink with Tasha's, who was looking around enthusiastically. Something told her that her house guest was going to be staying rather longer than she expected.

★   ★   ★

Mia sat back in her chair, one hand resting on her very full stomach, and watched in amazement as her little sister, so shy and unadventurous, kept pace with Alex's large family. You would think, she mused, that Tasha had been here as long as she had.

'More wine?' Alex said, taking his seat beside her and topping up his own glass.

'No thanks,' Mia said, as she continued to watch her sister. 'I need a clear head to write tomorrow.' Without realising it she found herself frowning.

'Am I to take it that you did not achieve your word count today?' he said softly, leaning back in his chair so they could talk privately. Mia raised an eyebrow.

'Not a word.' Then, realising how self-ish that sounded, she added, 'Not that I'm worried of course. It was lovely to see the sights and to spend some time with Tasha.'

'But?' Alex asked.

'I think she kind of likes it here, which is wonderful and I'm so glad she's safe. This place and this experience will be good for her ... ' Mia's voice trailed off as she wasn't certain she could put into words her competing emotions.

'It will be good for her, I think but for you, not so much.'

Mia looked at him to see if he was teasing but all she saw was a half-smile and understanding.

'I know I sound awful.'

Alex held up his hand.

'No Mia, not at all. You have a dream and you wish to follow it. There is nothing to be ashamed of in that. Have you spoken to your sister?'

'It doesn't really feel like a good time. It's not like I can say I'm so glad you're safe but when do you plan to leave?' Mia ran a hand through her hair. Her precious time here had been so short before her family, who seemed to be able to prevent her writing no matter where she was, got in the way? Even the thought itself made her blush and she was glad for once that she hadn't spoken it out loud. How could she be so selfish? If this was what writing brought out of her then maybe she should pack it in right now and go home.

'Perhaps all you need is some ground rules?' Alex suggested. 'She does not need to leave, but you need to set some time aside to write. I am sure you can find a compromise without upsetting her.'

Mia smiled, grateful once again for Alex's understanding, but wondering deep down if her baby sister had found an ability to compromise along with her adventurous streak!

9

The opportunity to raise the compromise issue did not arise after supper, mainly because Tasha had joined in a drinking game with two of Alex's younger cousins and so was in no fit state to do anything but roll into bed and then snore all night. Mia padded to the kitchen, made them both a cup of tea and then headed back to the double bed that they had shared.

'Tash,' she said softly, giving her shoulder a squeeze. 'Cup of tea if you want it.'

Mia was rewarded with a pillow-muffled groan and she wondered if perhaps the Greek tradition of coffee would have been more appropriate.

'I'm going to have a quick shower so speak now if you think you need to pee in the next five minutes.' Or anything else, she thought, wondering how bad Tasha's hangover might be. As the sounds of snoring had returned, Mia took that as a negative and headed towards the shower.

Mia had been writing for twenty-one minutes and had managed three hundred and forty-two words. Her concentration was broken when the cupboard doors in the kitchen area were opened and banged shut. Tasha was looking for something.

'Coffee,' Tasha said. 'I need coffee.'

'There should be some in the small cupboard over the sink,' Mia replied, refusing to take her attention away from her notebook in front of her; she was on a roll and didn't want to stop now. Tasha, surely, was capable of making herself a cup of coffee.

'Are you sure?' Tasha grumbled, as if Mia had gone out of her way to ensure that there would be no coffee, just when she was desperate for some.

'Yes, unless Alex has drunk it all. There's a little shop round the corner which should be open soon. My bag is by the door, help yourself to some euros and go get some.'

This last comment was greeted by what Mia could only assume was a stunned silence as she studiously avoided her sister's gaze.

'By myself?' Tasha said, as if Mia had suggested that she travel round the world independently.

'It's only a few minutes' walk, hon. Maybe the fresh air will do you good?'

Mia tried to think of the word that was to come next in the brilliant sentence she had just constructed in her brain, but it sailed away on the sea of distraction.

'Come with me?' Tasha said in a tone of voice that she had mastered at the age of three, one almost guaranteed to get her what she wanted, almost.

'Tasha, I'm trying to get a bit of writing in.' Mia gestured at her notebook as if somehow Tasha had managed to miss it.

'But you said it would only take a couple of minutes to get there.'

Mia sighed.

'And you need a break. Trying to write all day is not good for your creativity, you know.'

Mia could feel her resolve sag. It was probably easier, she thought, just to go with Tasha and get the coffee. Maybe then she could have a quick talk with her about Alex's compromise suggestion.

'Ok, although I've only been at it for half an hour and I planned to work for three.'

'The problem with you, Sis, is that you stick too rigidly to your plans. Sometimes you just need to be spontaneous,' Tasha said airily, before heading to the door and picking up Mia's bag.

Mia raised an eyebrow. Tasha had been spontaneous on only one occasion, which was the day before yesterday, and all of a sudden she was an expert. Forcing herself to think kind thoughts, Mia smiled.

'You're probably right. Why don't we go out for coffee, then we can have a chat.'

'Great!' Tasha said. 'I'm starving too, I could eat a horse!'

Mia wanted to say that she normally ate breakfast at home since she was on a fairly limited budget, but knew that now was not the time. Once Tasha had her coffee and something sweet she might be in a better frame of mind to receive Mia's latest plan.

★ ★ ★

'So, have you given any thought to what you're going to do whilst you're here?' Mia asked, a little tentatively.

Tasha shrugged. 'I've only just got here. I haven't had a chance to come up with a ten year life plan.'

'I wasn't thinking ten years, Tash, just wondering if there's anything you'd like to do.' Mia's mind drifted to her own plan and the fact that she was now two days out reminded her that she needed to redraft it, and quickly.

'Like what?'

'I don't know ... go see some sights, find something that you want to do, like my writing, or get some casual work.'

Tasha added yet another sachet of brown sugar into her half-drunk coffee.

'But I don't know what I want to do, that's why I left everything behind.'

94

Mia reached a hand across the table and gave Tasha's a squeeze.

'I know, hon, really, I understand. I'm just not sure you're going to find whatever it is by hanging around the flat all day, watching me scribble in my notebook.'

Mia resisted the urge to keep talking, allowing some silence to stretch between them and letting her words sink in.

'Perhaps I could help out Elizabeth at the taverna? She always seems to be rushed off her feet.'

Tasha looked really hopeful and Mia wasn't sure what to say. She didn't want to crush her first idea, but at the same time she wasn't sure she could bear for Tasha to ask Elizabeth for a job when she knew that they were only just getting by.

'I know that look,' Tasha said, not bothering to hide her irritation. 'I'm perfectly capable of clearing tables and taking food orders! It's not as if I didn't have a job at home.'

The job at home had been at the local supermarket where Tasha had joined as a Saturday day girl whilst still at school.

Once she had finished school she stayed on, but left once Tim proposed so that she could 'concentrate on planning the wedding and making a home'. Mia smiled.

'That's not what I was thinking at all, Tash. I'm sure you would be brilliant at it.' And it would certainly be good life experience, she thought to herself. 'It's just I think Elizabeth likes being busy, and besides I'm not sure they are looking for any help.'

Mia couldn't quite bring herself to tell Tasha the full story, it seemed disloyal somehow and she didn't want to remember the conversations she'd had with Alex as to why he had left University. The memory of that conversation was not one she wanted to dwell on, although she knew that they would need to talk about it at some point. For right now, though, she was just relieved that she had Alex as her friend. There would be time enough for more once she had sorted Tasha out and sent her back home.

Tasha was gazing out across the small square.

'Maybe I can just help out then. It's not like I'm going to be spending a lot of money whilst I am here and I have some savings I could use for paying my share, so don't worry about that.' She turned her head to look at Mia.

'I'm not completely helpless, Mia. I just wish everyone would realise that. And besides, Elizabeth said we were family, and family helps each other out.'

Tasha's voice was even but Mia wondered if she could hear a hint of reproach — or was it merely her own guilty conscience pricking at her? She couldn't be sure.

'Ok,' Mia said. 'Then how about I go back to the apartment and get on with my word count and you head over to the taverna?'

Tasha looked somewhat unimpressed by the suggestion.

'Elizabeth starts to bake about now,' Mia said looking at her watch. 'So I expect she could use some help.'

Tasha sipped at her coffee and played with the crumbs left over from her pastry on her plate.

'Don't you want me here?' Tasha asked in a voice that took Mia back to when they were children.

Mia took a deep breath and tried to force down the frustration she felt.

'Of course I do. It's lovely to see you and you know I like to spend time with you. It's just that I need to set some time aside to write. Tash, you know how important this is to me. You know how hard I had to save to be able to come here and not work for six months.'

Was Mia imagining it, or did Tasha's expression say that she knew Mia had worked hard — worked hard to get away from her family. That maybe Mia thought her writing was more important than her kin. Mia swallowed down the guilt. It wasn't true, she told herself firmly. She reached out for Tasha's hand and for a moment she worried that Tasha would pull back.

'Just give me a couple of hours,' Mia said quickly, as she wondered whether she could achieve her planned word count in that time. 'Then we can go out and do something together. Whatever you like.'

Tasha seemed to consider this, her face pouting just a little. She was making Mia wait, and Mia knew it, but she also knew her sister and there was nothing to be done but give her the time she was demanding.

'Ok then!' Tasha said, standing up and smiling, then gestured at the empty plates. 'You ok to get this?'

She didn't wait for an answer, just picked up her bag, waved distractedly and disappeared into the crowds that were headed towards the traditional market. With a sigh, Mia picked up the bill and carefully counted out her euros, wondering if what happened counted as a form of compromise.

10

Tasha's sudden appearance was now two weeks ago, but to Mia it felt like she had always been here. It was as if, when she had been planning her trip all those months ago at home, she had been sharing it with Tash, it had been their secret instead of hers alone. Mia had to admit that it was nice to have her sister around, nicer now that she had a focus to her everyday life. Elizabeth, at first reluctant to accept help for nothing, had finally agreed that Tasha could help out as and when she wanted to but made it clear that she was under no obligation to do so.

Mia stared at the blank page wondering where her muse had gone. The easy writing, where she would get lost and forget the time, seemed to have left her. Instead it was like a battle for every word and even when she did get words down they seemed to have lost the magic that she had been creating. Although Tasha was out from mid-morning till mid-afternoon and then again all evening, her presence seemed to bring back to Mia all that she had left behind and the worries and concerns for her family seemed to be more real. She knew it wasn't Tasha's fault; if anything, Tash had gone out of her way to be respectful of Mia's writing, which had certainly not been the case at home. But something had changed, and until she worked out what, she wasn't sure that she was going to achieve her goal of completing her first full novel.

Mia took a deep breath and rested her fingers on the page, trying to force all other thoughts from her mind and just write. But after what felt like hours, which turned out to be six minutes, she sighed and turned her attention to her mobile phone which had been curiously silent all morning. Alex must be busy with fares, she thought. She wondered if he would make it for lunch. Although she hadn't written more than a few hundred words, she hoped he would take pity on her and perhaps take her somewhere that would fire her imagination.

'I'm bored!' she texted him before she could change her mind. She forced herself to return to her pen and paper. The silence seemed oppressive and she knew that if she could just get an encouraging text or at least something to make her smile, like the promise of lunch, then she might just be able to focus and produce something half decent.

'Do you fancy lunch today?' she texted, but still nothing. She frowned. That was really unlike Alex; normally, even if he was busy, he would reply. Mia could feel it coming on, the worry — perhaps something was wrong, perhaps he had been in an accident? She tried to force her mind to calm down. This was exactly what happened at home, even when she did carve out some time to write. All the concerns and issues of her family used to crowd into her brain demanding their place and some attention. She sat back in her chair and stared at the wall. Alex was fine, she told herself firmly, you're being ridiculous.

She looked at her phone, telling herself that she just wanted to know what time it was. Eleven-thirty, it said, in stark bright blue numbers. How had so little time gone past? She looked up at the wall at her weekly planner. She was hopelessly behind to the point that she knew she was going to have to re-plan, something that she hated doing. She was clearly going to get nothing else done this morning just sat there. A cup of tea with Elizabeth might be just what she needed.

Turning the corner onto the small street where Alex's family lived and worked, she could hear loud voices, talking over each other, interspersed with laughter. She wondered why the family were there in the middle of the day, but then remembered it was Sunday. The family always gathered for lunch, after church. It was known to go on all day until supper time which is why Mia had never joined in. Walking up the steps to the terrace she could see the long family table in the corner was fully occupied.

'Mia, honey! We did not expect to see you in the daytime. Sit, sit. I will make us some tea.'

Elizabeth kissed her on both cheeks and Mia knew she had been right, this was what she needed. She might even talk to Elizabeth about how she was feeling. Elizabeth, like Alex, always seemed to know the right thing to say. As she grabbed a chair at the nearest end of the table, the conversation slowed enough for smiles and welcomes before returning their attention to their animated discussions.

A waving hand came from the other end of the table and Mia realised it was Alex. Tasha was sat next to him and was leaning in, whispering something in his ear. He turned his attention away from Mia after this cursory greeting and laughed warmly. Mia tried to fight it but couldn't. She felt the stab of jealousy run through her as if it were real, physical pain. Clearly he had been preoccupied with other things and so hadn't been checking his phone, even though Mia usually texted him around the same time every day with a progress report. She knew she was being unfair, in fact he was probably doing her a favour, keeping Tasha occupied so she could write. She felt a little burn of shame.

'Here you are, my darling,' Elizabeth said, before pulling a chair up to sit beside her, forcing Mia's attention away from Alex and her sister. Mia smiled her thanks.

'And how is it going today? I take it not so well since you have come here in search of company?' Elizabeth smiled, but there was something like concern in her eyes and Mia suddenly felt like she was going to cry. Elizabeth said nothing but reached out and squeezed Mia's hand, giving her time to compose herself.

'It's … Well, it's not going too well. I don't know what happened. I was being so productive and now all I do is stare at a blank page. I'm so behind I just don't know what to do … ' Mia knew she was rambling but didn't know how to stop herself.

'It's like I've lost my muse, left it some-where or maybe someone has stolen it.'

As she said those last words her eyes drifted unwillingly to the other end of the table to Alex and her sister, sat so closely together. Mia felt suddenly alone, as if she were not part of the family. As if Tasha had somehow assumed her place. Her hand flew to her mouth as she realised what she had said out loud and became aware that Elizabeth was watching her closely.

'I didn't mean that, of course. I'm just glad that Tasha is safe and well and it's lovely to see her ... ' Mia's voice trailed off as she wondered if she was trying to convince Elizabeth or herself.

'Family is hard,' Elizabeth said softly. Mia turned to stare at her, she had not expected Elizabeth to say such a thing. Elizabeth continued to speak.

'You love them, yes, you love your sister?'

Mia nodded, of course she did. They drove her crazy and sometimes it felt like her life was overwhelmed by them, but she loved them and knew how lucky she was to have them.

'As I love mine,' Elizabeth said, gesturing to the long table packed with people of all ages.

'Mine, I have married into. Yours you were born with, but whenever we have something good, whenever we have people to love and care for, we also have to deal with the negative side of that. And there always is one.' Elizabeth reached out for her glass and took a sip.

'We cannot have light without darkness, just as we cannot have love without pain. And I don't mean the pain of loss, but the pain that the people we love can cause as whilst they are still with us.

'My son gave up his future for his father and me. Our love caused that. If we did not love him as we do, if he did not love us as he does, he would have stayed away and followed his heart and his dreams, but instead he is tied to us by an invisible bond. Our love is both a gift and a curse. Once you accept that, well life can be a little easier.'

Mia watched as Elizabeth studied her son, who was oblivious to her gaze.

'Only a little, mind.' She smiled sadly. 'You had escaped all of this, both the good and the bad, and then suddenly your Natasha comes crashing back into your life and it's as if you never left. The real lesson, Mia my love, is to learn to write, or whatever it is that you dream of doing, in spite of them and the distractions they bring, both the good and the bad. You do not want to only be able to write when you are far from home, I think?'

Mia laughed. 'You are right of course, I just don't know how. I mean, Tasha walked away from everything. My mum phones every day worried about her, wondering if the wedding will happen, scared that Tasha will never go home.'

'Mothers worry, Mia. That is our lot in life! Just because your children are grown doesn't mean that you worry any less. But you are not Tasha's mother.'

Mia shook her head. 'I still feel responsible.'

'But she is a grown woman, no? She

seems happy and healthy. Perhaps the rest is for her to figure out. Has she asked your help in any of these things?'

'No,' Mia said, 'but she can't just ignore them!'

Elizabeth reached out and handed Mia the basket of bread that was doing the rounds.

'But she can! Perhaps you mean that *you* would not, but you and your sister are not the same person. She has her life to live and you must live yours. She will not thank you for interfering and you will only be distracted from your own life as you try to manage hers.'

Mia felt some of the tension fall away from her shoulders. Elizabeth was right, of course she was. Mia couldn't really blame Tasha for something that was really her own issue and all in her own mind. Tasha had come to Crete to find herself and Mia needed to let her.

'I have to go and start to prepare lunch, will you eat with us?'

Mia put her glass down with an air of determination.

'Actually, I think I might get back to it.'
Elizabeth smiled.

'Perhaps you will join us for supper? Then you can tell me all about your progress.'

Mia stood up and leaned in to kiss her friend.

'You really are the wisest, loveliest person I know.'

Elizabeth clicked her tongue and made shooing motions with her hands.

'It is always easy to be wise about someone else's problems, Mia. Now, if I could master my own … Well, then I would be truly wise.'

11

Mia leaned back in her chair and stretched out the crick in her neck, before carefully admiring the last tiny figure in her notebook, which told her how many words she had written. She crossed the room to her plan which hung Blu-Tacked to the wall, and ticked the word count for the day. Glancing at her watch she knew that she had missed supper, but it had been worth it. The words had flowed and she was feeling her muse again. Elizabeth had been right, the trick was not escaping all of the distractions, it was learning to write in spite of them. She hadn't thought about Tasha once all afternoon and evening, and actually found herself looking forward to hearing about her day, wondering what she had been up to.

Laughter filtered in from the street below and Mia made her way back to her desk where she could see the street below.

She had recognised the laughter straight away and it was good to hear Tasha sound happy. Mia moved the thin curtain aside, which she had pulled to block out the evening sun and froze. She had to blink as she could not take in what she was seeing. It felt like she was watching an old memory, one where she and Alex walked hand in hand down the narrow street, laughing and then ... Her brain could not form the words. It was no memory, however familiar it might seem, for she was not there — Tasha was. Mia felt as if her heart had stopped and then, as she watched, she felt as if it had shattered, along with the dream that had been her life for the past couple of months.

However much she wanted to step away, not to see what she knew in her heart was coming next, she couldn't. It was as if her brain could not communicate with her body, her legs would not obey. So instead she watched as Tasha, on her tiptoes, leaned in and kissed Alex. Alex, even his name caused a shock of pain, her Alex, that is how she thought of him. She knew they had argued before Tasha had arrived but surely it was just a disagreement, nothing they couldn't talk about and sort out? Did he really think it was over between them? And worse than that, could he so easily switch his affection to someone else? To her baby sister, no less.

She turned away, not wanting to see more. Her mind swirling with different emotions, she stepped away from the window, suddenly afraid that they would look up and see her watching. She felt slightly ashamed that she had watched such a private moment between them, but that was not the overriding emotion. Mia felt betrayed, by Alex of course, but worse, by Tasha. How could she do this? How could she not know that Mia and Alex were more than friends — or at least, Mia had thought they still were. Earlier today, she had given them the benefit of the doubt, ascribed motives to Alex that were about protecting her precious writing time. But now she knew differently. She had not factored into the situation at all.

Mia heard the heavy key in the front door downstairs and suddenly wanted to be anywhere other than the tiny apartment that she loved. One thing she knew for sure, she couldn't speak to Tasha or even look at her right now. She needed time to think, to pin down exactly how she felt. Mia scooped up her notebook and her grandmother's pen and crossed the room, stripping off her light cotton dress. She grabbed her pyjamas, pulled them on and threw herself into bed. She had just enough time to calm her breathing when the door to the apartment was pushed open.

Mia lay on her side, her face turned to the wall, and bit her lip to hold back the tears that were so close. She knew she could not cry as any movement at all might give away the fact that she was awake and Tasha would want to know what was wrong. Instead she focused all of her energy on being still. She listened as Tasha moved quietly around the apartment and eventually she fell into a fitful sleep.

* ★ ★

Mia could feel the misery well up inside her as the memory of the night before threatened to overwhelm her. She could hear Tasha's soft breathing in the bed beside her and so she slipped quietly out from under the covers and padded into the bathroom. Dressing quickly, she moved back into the main room and grabbed her notebook and bag. She wasn't sure she would be able to write a word, but she knew that she needed to be anywhere other than here. She forced herself to write Tasha a quick note saying that she needed a change of scene and so was going to find somewhere else to write. With a quick glance at her still-slumbering sister, she let herself out of the apartment.

Outside was deserted. Glancing at her watch, she realised it wasn't even seven o'clock, but the silence and stillness was all she felt she could cope with right now. Mia had no real plan as to where she was going, but she found that her feet were taking her down to the small harbour, where she had been many times with Alex. They would sit on the low sea wall, Alex would inevitably bring leftovers and they would eat an early breakfast together, watching the fishermen return from their night's work in their tiny, faded wooden fishing boats.

Mia flopped down onto the wall and stared out across the water. How could this have happened? She had never told Tasha that she and Alex were more than friends but surely that was obvious? And what about Tim? Tasha was supposed to be getting married! Her mind drifted and a memory of Alex filled it. What had always brought her such joy before now only seemed to bring pain. Had she been so wrong about him? But if he was the man she thought he was, then why was he kissing another girl so soon after their argument? It's not like they had ever discussed breaking up. The rational part of her brain managed to fight through the emotions and remind her that they had never really talked about what they were to each other, so maybe she was being unfair.

A figured appeared beside her. Mia used her hand to shield her eyes from the early morning sun but the figure remained in shadow.

'Good morning, Mia.'

Alex's voice made her jump just a little. She felt as if her memory had suddenly come to life and things were as they had been.

'Morning,' Mia managed to say, her manners not quite forgotten.

'I did not expect to see you here this morning. Did we make arrangements that I have forgotten?' He sounded so normal, so like her Alex in that moment that she could almost believe she had dreamt the events of last night.

'Is everything ok?' he asked as he sat beside her. Now she could see his face clearly and it was crumpled in concern.

Mia opened her mouth, fully intending to say that she'd woken early and fancied a change of scenery; instead she blurted,

'How could you kiss my sister?'

In normal circumstances, Mia would have been embarrassed to spill out her feelings so readily, but the hurt and anger had made her bolder than she realised. After a moment to recover herself she looked him in the eye and saw only bemusement and she felt ice in her veins. She had her answer. He didn't even have the grace to look embarrassed at being caught out. Mia turned her face away. If this was a game to him there was no way she was going to give him the satisfaction of seeing how much he had hurt her.

'Mia, it was nothing,' he said. His smile was so natural that it almost made her feel as if she was overreacting — but only almost. That thought made her angry and she glared at him.

'Really Mia, I thought you would be pleased that I was taking Natasha around the island, showing her the sights as I did for you, keeping her occupied so that you could write.'

'Keeping her occupied?' Mia said, her

voice suddenly high-pitched. 'Making her fall in love with you, more like.'

Mia could hear her words in her ears and knew that she sounded crazy, hysterical even.

'Mia, please,' Alex said, reaching out to rest a hand on her arm but she shook herself free. His touch, so welcome before, now felt alien to her, like she couldn't bear to be near him.

'Mia, you must listen to me. Tasha and I are just friends, that is all that either of us want.'

'Really?' Mia said shouting now. 'And have you spoken to my sister about this? Because I think I know her better than you do, and I can tell you right now that she is falling in love with you.'

Alex looked torn between being amused and bemused. He tried a smile but that only made Mia more angry. How could he be so calm and dismissive? If Tasha thought Alex loved him then there was sure to be serious trouble ahead and as usual Mia would have to pick up the pieces. Mia would be the one who would have to listen to Tasha sobbing, not Alex, and all the while she would be nursing her own broken heart.

'Mia, please be reasonable.'

That was the last straw. Not trusting herself to say anymore on the subject, she stood up and strode away down the ancient promenade, with the sound of Alex calling her name ringing in her ears.

12

Mia wandered around the streets, not wanting to go home or to the taverna, waiting for the village to wake up. What she wanted more than anything was a comforting cup of tea and something to eat. Despite her upset, her stomach rumbled, reminding her that she had skipped supper the night before and now she was very hungry. She found herself near the apartment complex that she had shared for one night with the local holiday reps and beside it found the small café, which she knew was run by an English couple who had retired to Crete a few years before. Everything about it screamed English and Mia felt a sudden wave of homesickness. Each table was carefully laid out with a bright red gingham tablecloth, tea pots lined one wall and signs advertised a full English breakfast and home-cooked meals.

She sat down at one of the tables outside and then thought better of it. The café was on one of the main roads, which Alex frequently travelled on his way to the airport, and he was the last person she wanted to see right now. So she walked inside and sat herself at a table away from the window, where she felt she would be reasonably well hidden from passers-by. She needed to think about something other than Alex and Tasha and so she fished out her notebook and pen.

'Morning love, what can I get you?' Mia looked up and the warm smile almost made her cry. The owner was grey-haired, tanned and tall, and despite the heat wore the obligatory white socks with his open-toed sandals. He was the spitting image of her dad when he was on holiday.

'Tea, please and a full English. Thank you.'

'One taste of home coming right up,' the owner said, before disappearing through the beaded curtain that led to the kitchen.

'Mia? Mia Bowman?'

Mia jumped at the sound of her name but her heart slowed as her brain processed the accent, which was not Greek or English, but instead, American. She looked up and saw the man who had rescued her from a trip around the luggage carousel at the airport. She searched her memory for his name.

'Mr Evans,' she said with a smile.

'Parker, please. How is your stay in Crete so far, Mia?' he asked as he collected up his bag and coffee and sat down beside her. Mia allowed herself to smile inwardly at the fact that he had even thought to ask, and before she knew it she was blurting out everything about her writing, and her family, before concluding, with a rueful smile: 'It's not too bad, all in all, although now my sister has come over, that's a bit of a distraction.' She hoped he wouldn't ask for any details, as she really didn't feel like sharing any more of that particular story. Parker Evans nodded in complete understanding.

'That, my dear, is a common problem, but I do have a suggestion that might help you out, if you're interested?'

Right now, Mia thought, she would have accepted a night out in the town that was tourist party central, if it could help as a distraction from her current woes.

'You see, I run writing summer schools here on the island,' Parker said, taking a sip of coffee as Mia's breakfast and much longed for cup of tea arrived. 'You know the sort of thing, people come from all over the world for an intensive week of writing. We provide accommodation and food so there aren't too many distractions. We share what we write so there's plenty of feedback to be had. Most people find it a really useful creative space.'

Mia took a mouthful of tea, hardly able to believe the coincidence. She wondered how things would have worked out if she had only mentioned to Parker the first time she met him her reasons for coming to Crete. She started her breakfast, partly to calm her rumbling belly and partly to give her time to think.

'I'm not sure I could intrude,' Mia said finally, although she had to admit the idea was tempting.

'You wouldn't be!' Parker said loudly. 'We have plenty of room.'

Mia mentally checked her bank balance. She had looked into writing retreats before, and decided they were outside of her means.

'If I'm honest, I can't really afford it. It's not as if I have a job and the money I have saved needs to last me another four months.'

Mia could feel Parker studying her and so she focused on her breakfast.

'Well, how about I make you a deal? Presumably you have somewhere to stay, so you wouldn't need accommodation. That's probably the most expensive bit, along with the flights.'

Mia looked up. Parker seemed to embody the word 'creative'. He was dressed, as before, in a loose white linen shirt, crumpled as if he didn't have the time to waste ironing, pale khaki baggy trousers and flip-flops that had seen better days.

His enthusiasm for writing might be just what she needed right now, to get back on track and to help her forget about Alex and Tasha.

'The group that arrive on Sunday are the beginner's course and I could do with some help. We run individual tutorials and group sessions. If you could help me out with those, I'm sure we can squeeze you into the advanced course on the week after.'

'I'm not sure that I would know what to do in a tutorial,' Mia said.

'You just read what they've written, talk to them about structure and plot. You'd be great, I'm sure.'

Mia leaned back in her chair and glanced out the window. Maybe helping others with their writing could help her. It certainly would give her the change of scene that she needed.

'And if you need any further tempting, we have a couple of published authors coming on the advanced course.'

Mia turned back to Parker suddenly

and saw the glint in his eyes. Published authors were like the Holy Grail to unpublished writers. Published authors meant agents and contacts, people who could help you achieve your goal.

Inside she could feel the tug of her plan, carefully laid out with what she would do every day of her stay, hung on the wall of the apartment. It was like she could feel its disapproval from where she sat. It was so unlike her, but she had an overwhelming urge to tear it up into tiny pieces and throw it in the bin. Where had it got her so far? Certainly not where she wanted to be and now she was being offered a fantastic opportunity and she was going to take it.

'I'm sold,' Mia said, with a smile.

'Fantastic! You're a life saver, Mia, and I'm sure you'll get a lot out of it. You never know, it might be just what you need.'

An image of Alex and Tasha swam into Mia's mind and she had to agree with him. After scribbling down her address on a paper napkin for Parker, he left her to it, promising to pick her up early Sunday morning so he could drive her to the villa where the course would be run.

Encouraged by the friendly owners to stay in the café as long as she liked, Mia got out her notebook and managed to focus on her writing, whilst being supplied with a steady stream of tea, until late afternoon. When she arrived back at her apartment she found a note from Tasha, saying she had gone to help Elizabeth set up, but that Mia should come down and join them when she could. Elizabeth, the note said, insisted. It was not good for Mia to keep going without meals.

Mia took her time having a shower and getting changed. If all the family were there as usual then she would likely not even have the opportunity to talk to Tasha or Alex. And anyway, she didn't like to feel as if she was being chased away from seeing Elizabeth and the rest of the family. They were part of her life too! She could be an adult about this, and more than anything she wanted to share her exciting news with Elizabeth, who had become like a second mum to her.

Mia had timed it perfectly. The family were all seated at the table and the noise levels were high, news was being exchanged and although it stopped briefly to welcome her, Mia was able to slip into the seat next to Elizabeth. One quick glance and she could see that Tasha and Alex were sat at the far end, loudly sharing a joke with two of Alex's cousins.

'Mia, darling. We've missed you,' Elizabeth said, before pulling Mia into a seated hug. 'It is not good for you to eat alone. In Crete, we eat together, as family.'

Mia smiled.

'I'm sorry, but I've been getting a bit caught up in my writing and so didn't notice the time.'

Elizabeth seemed to be somewhat placated by this and she smiled.

'Well that is good too, of course, but Mia, you must eat!'

And with that she stood up and bustled out to the kitchen to start bringing out the laden trays of food. Mia stood up and followed her, meaning to help but also hoping to be able to tell her about the writing course.

'Mia, you should sit! What are you doing in here?'

'I came to help, of course,' Mia said with a smile, and she reached out for the two baskets of fresh bread. Elizabeth reached over and slapped her hand away.

'Go, sit! You have been working all day. You do not come her to wait on family.'

'I've been writing, Elizabeth, something I love, so it's not exactly work and anyway, you are waiting on family so why shouldn't I help?'

'Tsh!' Elizabeth said, but Mia could tell that she wasn't really cross.

'And besides I have something to tell you. I met this man at the airport when I arrived.'

Elizabeth stopped what she was doing and gave Mia her attention.

'Nothing like that,' Mia said, with a giggle. 'It turns out he's a fellow writer and he has invited me to help out on a beginners' writing course that starts at the weekend. In return, I'm going to attend his advanced writers' course.'

Elizabeth's face broke into a smile and she walked to Mia. Putting a hand gently to each side of her face she said, 'Mia, that is wonderful news! A real opportunity, I think. Who is this mysterious man that you met at our airport?'

'He's American, or at least I think he is by his accent. I never really asked,' Mia said with a brief frown. 'His name is Parker ... '

Mia didn't get to finish her sentence as a voice behind her spoke her last word.

'Evans? Parker Evans? Mia, you should stay away from this man.'

Mia knew without turning that it was Alex. She fought to get her emotions in check. He had no right to tell her what to do! How dare he? She could feel Elizabeth studying her face. Elizabeth reached for the baskets of bread, stepped carefully around Mia and quietly left the kitchen.

13

It took Mia a few moments to find her voice.

'I'm pretty sure it's nothing to do with you, Alex. I don't need to ask your permission, for anything.' In her head, she added, it's not as if you have asked for mine!

Alex seemed a bit taken aback by the coldness of her words but in that moment Mia didn't care. She had been angry and hurt before, seeing him so quickly find someone else, and her little sister no less, but now she was furious. This was a great opportunity for her to move forward with her dream and Alex wasn't going to stop her.

'I am just looking out for you, Mia. This man, he has a reputation on this island, one that is well known.'

'Really?' Mia said. She knew she was glaring now and she was also fairly sure that he had no idea why she was so mad! 'I don't think, under the circumstances, you have any right to say anything about another man's behaviour, do you?'

Alex sighed and Mia felt it was exaggerated.

'Really Mia, I thought we had discussed this. It was nothing. This is Greece, we kiss, and we are friendly. It does not mean what you think it means.'

Alex took a step towards her but Mia couldn't bear to be any nearer to him, she was almost afraid she would lash out.

'You might want to speak to my sister about that,' she said, feeling a flash of sisterly concern. 'She is really vulnerable right now and I can't believe you would take advantage of her like that. I thought I knew you.'

Mia stopped talking. Alex looked as if she had slapped him across the face. There was colour in his cheeks and Mia wondered if for the first time she would see him lose his temper. She watched wordlessly as a battle raged across his face but as quickly as it started it was gone, replaced with a blankness that scared her more. She felt the last bit of hope that their relationship could be salvaged, die.

'I am sorry that you think so little of me Mia. I will stay out of your affairs as instructed.'

He turned away from her and she had to fight the urge to call out to him and apologise. She hated to fight, hated to see someone else in pain but the anger inside her would not quiet enough to let her find the words. He pushed at the swing door and paused.

'You have made your decision, that is obvious, but I think perhaps we should let Natasha make up her own mind.' He looked at her now and his gaze was level, as if he had just asked her what she wanted to drink.

'Of course,' Mia said, feeling like she couldn't really say anything else after her outburst.

The kitchen door swung in and out. With each swing, she could hear the sounds of the family, happy and together, and she felt the loneliness from earlier return. She could not see herself sitting down to eat with them now but also didn't see how she could escape without appearing extremely rude. She stayed rooted to the spot with no idea what to do and then Elizabeth returned. On her face Mia saw concern, and she felt the tears threaten again. She opened her mouth to speak, not knowing what to say. Elizabeth held up her hands.

'You do not need to tell me, Mia my love. A lovers' tiff, it is better kept between the lovers, I think?' Elizabeth smiled kindly and pulled her in to a quick tight hug. 'Now, we had best feed the family or I fear there will be a riot.' With one hand she picked up a plate of stuffed peppers and with her other reached out for Mia's hand.

'Come, whatever has been said, still you must eat!'

Mia allowed herself to be pulled back out into the restaurant.

★   ★   ★

Mia heard the door to the apartment open. She had left soon after eating, claiming to be tired. She had thought about going to bed and pretending to be asleep, but she knew she couldn't avoid Tasha forever, so instead she made herself some tea and sat reading what she had written that day. The door clicked and Mia looked up.

'Want some tea?' she said, feeling quite pleased that she had managed to say the words in a pleasant tone.

'No, but I'd like an explanation.'

Tasha was standing just in front of the closed door, arms tightly crossed and an expression that could only be described as thunderous. Mia drained the last of her tea and moved to the kitchen to click the switch on the kettle.

'For what, Tash?' There, again she had managed to keep her voice light.

'Why are you being so mean to Alex?'

Mia turned from making her tea and fought to keep her temper in check. Why was it that family knew exactly what to say to wind you up?

'I'm not being mean to Alex, Tasha.' She kept her voice level with effort.

'Then why was he so upset this evening?'

'I don't know. Maybe you should ask him.'

Tasha dropped her bag and walked into the kitchen.

'Look, I know your relationship is none of my business, but anyone can see that Alex has been good for you. I mean, you looked so happy when you were together. He seems like a good guy.'

This seemed like the height of hypocrisy to Mia, after all Tasha had kissed him, or been kissed by him. Whatever had happened, she doubted that Tasha was entirely innocent.

'You mean like Tim?'

Mia watched as Tasha had the good grace to blush.

'That's different.'

'Is it?' Mia asked, raising an eyebrow as she sipped at the hot tea.

'Tim and I, it's complicated.' With a sigh, Tasha sat down in one of the rickety chairs at the kitchen table. Mia felt a flash of guilt at doing to Tasha exactly what Tasha had done to her.

'You can talk to me about it, you know,' Mia said, the anger fading to be replaced with the all-too-familiar concern for her baby sister.

'I've been with him for so long, you know? I've never had another boyfriend.'

Mia nodded to show she understood, not wanting to interrupt now that Tasha had started to speak.

'It just suddenly struck me that I'm in my early twenties and my life has already been mapped out. I mean, it's been mapped out since I was a kid. I feel stuck, like I'm never going to be able to change.'

Tasha shrugged helplessly and Mia reached out to squeeze her hand.

'It's like I'm having a midlife crisis, really, really early.'

Mia had to laugh now and Tasha joined her with a rueful smile.

'You don't have to do anything you don't want to. And you should definitely take time to figure out what it is that you want. But don't wait too long … '

'I know, it's not fair on Tim and I worry that he might meet someone else or just not want me anymore.'

Mia saw the warning signs of tears and leaned over and pulled Tasha into a hug.

'Do you still love him?' she asked quietly.

Mia could feel Tasha nod as she started to sob. She rubbed Tasha's back and tried to find the words to ask the question she wanted to ask.

'Honey, is there someone else?' Mia steeled herself. She knew she was pushing for an answer and it wasn't all about concern for Tasha, but she needed to know. Tasha pulled away from Mia so quickly, with a look of shock on her face.

'Of course not! Like who?'

'I don't know,' Mia shrugged. 'Someone from home?' She'd wanted to say someone from here, but couldn't quite bring herself to do so.

'No, there's no one else.' Tasha stood and turned away from Mia. She seemed suddenly to want a hot drink and she busied herself making it.

Mia knew when her sister was lying or at least feeling guilty. Avoidance was Tasha's MO in these situations, it always had been, even when she was a little girl. Mia felt a stab of pain, she had been right about the kiss, about Alex. It was so clear in Tasha's actions now.

'Maybe I should talk to Tim,' Tasha said, without turning round.

'Maybe you should,' Mia said.

There had been a small part of her that had believed what she had seen was a mistake, or that Alex was right, it was just how things were in Greece: people kissed, but it didn't mean anything. What hurt most right now was the fact that he had lied about it so brazenly. He looked her in the face and lied. Then he had looked hurt when she had called him on it. At the time she had wondered whether she had really upset him, whether she had got it completely wrong, but now she knew differently. She had been played. Alex was not really interested in her. Maybe it was all a game, a sport to him?

'Why don't you sleep on it?' Mia said, standing and moving towards the bathroom. 'I don't know about you but it's been a long day.'

Mia wanted, needed to stop talking. She was afraid of what she might say or how she might lash out.

'Mia? Thanks for listening.' Tasha looked so young and uncertain that Mia had to smile just a little. 'I know me turning up has kind of messed with your plans. I just didn't know where else to go and I had to get away.'

Mia had a flash of memory to her five-year-old sister, confessing to dropping Mia's favourite book in the bath. She crossed the space between them and pulled Tasha in to a hug.

'I'm glad you came, Tash.' And Mia knew that she meant it, despite all that had happened. 'It doesn't matter where I am or what I'm doing, I'll always be there for you.'

Mia wondered if she should tell Tasha that she had seen her kiss Alex, wondered if she should warn her that Alex was not who he appeared to be. She was her big sister and it was her job to protect her.

'I'm glad I came too,' Tasha said. 'And I may be the little sister here but you know you can talk to me too, about Alex, about anything.'

'I know that,' Mia said, and managed a smile, even though she knew that talking to Tasha about how she felt about Alex was probably not a good idea.

14

Despite Mia's best intentions she found it hard to keep her mind off Alex. The last angry conversation kept playing in her head. One moment she had convinced herself that his hurt was genuine and that she had been totally wrong, and the next she had convinced herself she was a fool: this was what Alex did, he worked his magic on the tourists and romanced them for a while before moving on to the next, like some strange game. Then she would think of Elizabeth and be back to the start, she was wrong about Alex.

'Mia?' The voice cut through her day-dreams and she guiltily sat up straighter. She was here to work, not moon over a boy, especially one who'd kissed her sister.

'I'm sorry,' she said. 'I got a little distracted.'

The small group who sat around the table smiled, they were all so different but they had one thing in common — they all wanted to write.

'The muse can strike at any time, people,' Parker said, waving his arms around extravagantly. The six women in the group all giggled appreciatively. One thing Mia was sure of was that Parker loved his job.

'I was actually asking if you wanted a coffee before we leave these good people to their nightly writing exercise.'

'Oh, no, thank you.'

Parker pushed himself away from the long wooden table that they all sat round.

'In that case, my friends, we will leave you to it. We'll meet out on the veranda tomorrow at ten, and remember, tomorrow you will need to read out tonight's task, so get writing.'

Mia stood and followed Parker off the wide wooden veranda that served as the evening meeting place. Parker opened the door to his fairly elderly car and Mia sank into the seat. Writing was tiring but helping new writers was more so. You had to work hard to get the balance right between being honest and damaging their self-esteem.

'So, are you having fun?' Parker asked, as he eased the car out onto the deserted narrow road that led from the large villa complex to the main road, which would take Mia home. Mia answered with a wide yawn that seemed to come out of nowhere. Parker laughed warmly.

'It's not as easy as writing yourself, is it?' he said.

'Not at all, but I have to say I'm kind of enjoying it.'

'You wait till next week. This week feels like a challenge but next week is something else altogether. Next week you'll need to bring your A game.'

Mia nodded. Despite the lack of street lighting, the moon was full and high in the sky, and she knew that Parker could see her.

'So, I was thinking, maybe we could do dinner at the end of the week? The course members fly home on Friday and the new guests don't arrive until Sunday, so perhaps Saturday? We could compare notes and I could give you a few pointers.'

Mia looked over to study Parker's face. Unbidden, Alex's warning about him popped into her mind. Alex had suggested that Parker was a player and that his reputation preceded him. The thing was, the warning didn't seem to fit at all with the man who had given her such a great opportunity.

'No pressure if you have plans,' Parker added, mildly, like he wasn't worried either way. Mia thought for a moment.

'No, I've no plans. Dinner would be lovely.' Alex had no right to judge anyone else after what he had done.

'Perfect. How about I pick you up at nine? I know a great little taverna up in the mountains with fantastic views. It's kind of out of the way, so it's usually tourist-free.' He grinned now and Mia grinned back, even though a tiny voice in her head told her she needed to be careful.

Mia stepped out of the car and waved as Parker drove off. Turning towards the shared door to the apartment, she realised that someone was sat on the bottom step. The tall buildings blocked out some of the moonlight and Mia couldn't make out who it was. She moved slowly, finding the key in her bag so that she had some sort of weapon if she needed it, and squinted trying to see who it was.

'Hello?' she said softly. The figure was resting its head on its knees but Mia felt sure it was a man. 'Are you ok?' she tried, which she knew was probably not going to help as it was likely that the man was Greek and may not speak English.

'Tash?' the voice said, and Mia knew who it was. She moved quickly to the figure who looked so lost.

'Tim? It's Mia. Are you ok?' Stupid question, she thought, but she had to say something.

'Tasha's not here,' Tim said, and Mia could feel his misery roll off him in waves.

'She is here, Tim, and she's fine. She's helping out at a local restaurant and people eat late here. She'll be home soon, I'm sure.'

Mia reached out a hand to Tim.

'Come on,' she said. 'Let's go upstairs. You look like you could do with a cup of tea and something to eat. We can wait for Tash upstairs.'

Tim stared at the hand for some time, with the look of fatigue that was familiar to all travellers. Eventually, he reached up, and Mia hauled him to his feet. She pushed the key in the lock but the sound of laughter made her pause. She pushed the door open, hoping that Tim was so locked in his own world that he wouldn't notice, but she was wrong. Mia turned and wondered what she could say that might make this moment better but knew there was nothing. So instead she stood beside him as they watched Alex and Tasha make their way down the narrow street, completely oblivious once again to who was watching them.

Mia didn't need to be a mind reader to know what Tim was thinking, it was painfully obvious merely by looking at his face. She willed Tasha to look over, to see him, to tone down her behaviour, but she didn't. Tasha seemed too lost in having a good time with Alex to notice anyone else. Mia noticed that Tim had clenched his fists and now she was worried that there would be a fight. She knew Tim would never hurt Tasha, and up to that moment she would have said that Tim didn't have a violent bone in his body. But she also knew what it felt like to see the person you love with someone else, especially when it was the last thing you were expecting to see.

Mia reached out for Tim's arm and he looked at her, surprised, as if he had forgotten that she was there.

'Who is that?' Tim asked, his voice almost begging for an explanation.

'That's our friend, Alex.' She knew she was labouring the words 'our friend' in the hope that he would accept them, despite the events that were playing out before him. 'His parents own the restaurant where Tasha has being helping out. I expect Alex just thought Tasha shouldn't walk home alone.'

Tim tore his eyes away from the two figures to glance at Mia briefly and she knew that she had not been able to convince him that what he was seeing was entirely innocent. But then, she couldn't blame him, since she had felt exactly the same way. Even though seeing Tasha and Alex together wasn't a shock to Mia this time, it still felt like a kind of betrayal and so she could only imagine what Tim was feeling, seeing the woman he thought he was going to marry, arm in arm with another man.

Together, they waited and watched. Tasha's steps faltered as she realised that she and Alex were not alone. For a moment she paused and simply stared, and then she unlinked her arm from Alex and started to run. A few steps from Tim and she faltered again, finally seeing the look on his face.

'Tim?'

Her voice sounded so small and she seemed so young in that moment that Mia wished she could protect her from the pain that was undoubtedly about to follow. Tim didn't say anything, he just stared and folded his arms. When Tasha made to move towards him, he took a step back, sending out the message loud and clear.

'It's good to see you, Tim,' Tasha tried again.

'Is it?' Tim asked, his voice cold.

Tasha looked bereft. 'Of course it is! I've missed you. I ... ' Tasha's voice tailed off and unconsciously she looked over her shoulder to where Alex was standing a few feet away. Tasha looked back at Tim and Mia could see all the pieces fall together in Tasha's mind.

'It's not what you think, Tim. This is my friend, Alex.' Tasha gestured to Alex who carefully stepped forward and offered Tim his hand. Tim tensed and so did Mia. Tim ignored the hand.

'I flew all this way to tell you I understood how you were feeling. So that we could talk and make new plans. But I can see you already have your new life figured out, and apparently it doesn't include me.'

Tasha was shaking her head vigorously.

'That's not true, Tim. All the time I've

151

been here, I've been thinking about you and about us …'

Tim cut her off with a dismissive hand.

'Not enough to pick up the phone, though,' he said. 'Or even send a text, just to let me know that you were ok. Instead, I have to find out all that from your mum, Tash.' The anger on Tim's face was being replaced by deep hurt.

'I'm sorry, Tim, really I am. I thought you would be angry with me for just leaving and I needed time to … ' Again Tasha's voice trailed off. Tim laughed but it was harsh and there was no humour to it.

'That's just the thing, Tasha. I wasn't angry. I wished you'd told me how you were feeling. If you had, you might have realised that I was feeling that way too. I could deal with all that. But this.' Tim waved his hand in Alex's direction. 'This, Tasha?' He shook his head. 'You've been gone less than three weeks and you've met someone else. You were the love of my life.' Tim's voice seemed to have stalled and it was clear to Mia that he was fighting tears. She reached an arm out for his.

'Tim, you've had a long day. Why don't you come inside, have something to eat? We can all get some sleep and talk about this in the morning?'

One look at Tim's face and Mia knew that there was no chance of that.

'Thanks Mia, very kind, but I don't think it would be a good idea. I can't be around your sister right now. I'm going to go back to the airport, to get the first flight home I can.' He glanced at Tasha. 'I shouldn't have come.'

'Tim, please,' Tasha said, and now she was sobbing. Mia wondered for a second if Tim would be won over. He had always hated to see Tasha upset, but she watched as, with effort, he set his face. He leaned in to kiss Mia on the cheek.

'Thank you,' he whispered, and then he was gone, striding off up the street.

'Tim!' Tasha called, and made to run after him, but Mia grabbed her arm.

'You need to let him go,' Mia said softly. 'Tash, he's angry right now. Let him calm down.'

'I can't let him just leave, not with things like this between us. I need to talk to him, to tell him.' Her voice cracked and then Mia was holding her sobbing sister in her arms.

Mia looked over her sister's head to Alex. No words passed between them, but Mia knew her face was reproachful, that her expression said that this was at least partly his fault. Alex nodded. Whether he was saying he understood or if he was saying that she was right, Mia couldn't tell. Alex turned and walked away. Mia watched him go before half-carrying her distraught sister upstairs and into their apartment.

15

Mia watched the sunrise through the delicate muslin curtains that hung at the window overlooking the street below. Tasha had finally cried herself to sleep an hour ago. Mia felt the tiredness claw at her but she had been unable to calm her mind enough to give in to it. There were too many thoughts screaming for attention and she had not been able to settle to anything, so instead she had made endless cups of tea and waited for the sun to rise. Movement from the small figure in the bed drew her attention away from the glimmer of golden rays. Mia waited, but Tasha merely sighed and turned over.

Mia picked up her phone again, wondering if she should text Tim. Part of her thought she should stay out of it. It was between Tim and Tasha and they were both grown-ups — but Tasha had been so distraught last night, Mia couldn't ignore the sense that perhaps she could at least bring them together so they could talk about it. Was that interfering or was that just being a good older sister? Mia wasn't sure.

Her eyes wandered over to her plan. She stood and walked over to the large sheet of white paper that hung on the wall. She had made the necessary adaptations to compensate for the writing course this week and next, but right now she couldn't imagine writing a single word or concentrating on supporting her students. Then she knew she had made her decision. She might not be able to fix Tasha's relationship with Tim, but she could at least bring them together. Perhaps if she did that she could return her energies to her writing.

With one last glance at her sleeping sister, she grabbed her bag and her phone and silently let herself out of the apartment. The street outside was quiet and deserted except for one car, which she recognised instantly. She walked slowly towards it, wondering why Alex had left it there. Peeking in the window, she saw Alex, complete with a five o'clock shadow which suggested he had not been home, fast asleep. His head leaning against the driver's side window and his legs stretched out across the passenger seat. Her heart did the all-too-familiar leap at the sight of him, but the recent memories of their fight kept the smile from her face. As if on cue, Alex jerked, almost as if he knew he was being watched. He rubbed a hand across his face before he saw Mia at the window.

Alex moved so that he was sat in the driver's seat and indicated that she should get in. For a split second Mia thought about refusing, but the truth was she was too tired to get into another argument. Plus, although she hated to admit it, she was a little curious as to what he was doing there.

'Don't you have a bed you can sleep in?' Mia asked, trying to hide the smile at Alex's sheepish expression. He did look as if he had been caught doing something he shouldn't.

'I just wanted to be close by in case you needed me,' he said. He didn't look at her. Mia shook her head in amusement.

'What did you think we would need you for?'

Alex shrugged, and with some effort turned to face her.

'Tasha's partner seemed pretty angry. I thought maybe I should be close by, just in case.'

Mia raised an eyebrow.

'He was pretty mad but I'm not sure that your presence would have helped that.'

'There is nothing going on between me and Tasha,' he said firmly, but Mia was sure she could see a look of pleading in his eyes. She took a moment to study his face. Her heart wanted to believe him but her head was having none of it.

'That may be, Alex, but that's not the impression either of you are giving out to the rest of the world.' Mia was ashamed to admit that she felt somewhat vindicated in her own reaction now that she had seen Tim's. Alex sighed and ran a hand through his sleep tousled hair with frustration.

'How is Tasha?'

'Upset,' Mia said gently. Alex raised an eyebrow. 'Ok, she's distraught, but she's finally asleep.'

'I never meant for this to happen. Tasha and I, we are just very good friends.'

Mia watched as his gaze transferred to the small window on the second floor.

'Will she forgive me?' he said softly. Mia reached out a hand for him, feeling her heart winning out over her head.

'I don't think there is anything to forgive you for, Alex. You can't give out the impression you did last night on your own. Tasha had a part to play in it all and I think she knows that. You both may have agreed that there was nothing going on between you, but that's not how it felt to me, or to Tim.'

Alex nodded but said nothing. They sat in silence for a while and Mia wondered if she should say something more, if there was something that could get her and Alex back to where they had been before Tasha arrived. But there was part of her that was not ready to accept his explanation, at least not yet.

'Why are you out and about so early?' Alex asked. 'You don't have your notebook so I think that writing is not on your agenda.'

Now it was Mia's turn to shrug. 'I thought maybe I would go and see if I could find Tim. I don't have to be at the course until ten.' Mia glanced at her watch, it was a few minutes after seven.

'Where do you think he will be? There are plenty of places a tourist can hide on this island,' Alex said. If he was surprised at her plans, he didn't say anything.

'The last thing he said was that he was going to get the first flight home, so I thought I would try the airport.'

'Did you plan to walk?' Alex said, and Mia saw him smile just a little.

'I hadn't really got as far as working that bit out.'

Alex laughed then, and Mia felt the

smallest hint of warm glow return to her.

'You mean you did not have a comprehensive plan worked out? Mia I am shocked.'

Mia elbowed him in the side and glared.

'I don't plan everything, you know.'

Alex raised a sceptical eyebrow but said, 'Well, perhaps I can help you out. I have to collect a family whose flight gets in at nine. I can at least drive you there.'

'Thanks. I just thought maybe I could persuade him to come back with me and at least talk to Tasha.'

Mia could see that Alex was fairly doubtful of her chances of success.

'I can at least try,' she said, knowing she sounded desperate. 'The fact that they are both so upset must mean that there is still something to be saved.'

'I'm sure you are right,' Alex said, before starting the engine. 'And as you said, you can at least try.' Not exactly the encouragement that Mia was looking for, but it would have to do.

The airport seemed to be just waking up. There were no customers, but plenty of workers. Rows of coaches were parked along the road that led to the arrivals area and alongside them were the accompanying holiday reps in bright, holiday camp-style blazers and clipboards. They were mainly standing around, drinking coffee, which was no surprise to Mia since she had shared accommodation with them for one night and knew that all the partying stories were true. Mia scanned the crowds but they all seemed to know exactly where they were going. Tim was not among them.

'Do you see him?' Alex asked, keeping his eye on the traffic, which was a little unpredictable at the airport, with cars and taxis dropping off and picking up.

'No. I think I should get out and look in the terminal. He didn't say he had a flight booked, so I guess he might be on standby.' Mia knew that this was a bit like looking for a needle in a haystack.

'I'll park up and come find you,' Alex

said, pulling the car into the parking lane.

'Not sure that's a great idea,' Mia said doubtfully. She wasn't sure that Tim would be ready to listen to her as it was, but she was certain he wouldn't if Alex was with her.

'As soon as we've found him, I'm gone, but if he is not here I can at least drop you at a bus stop that will take you home. You don't want to be late for your course.'

Mia looked at him sharply but there was no sign that he was making a pointed comment.

'Thanks, actually that would be good.'

Mia gave her eyes a moment to adjust to the move from bright early sun to dim interior. She did a quick visual check but couldn't spot Tim. The first flight seemed to have arrived and the wide, high-roofed area that served as both arrivals and departures was a sea of tired, slightly confused-looking people. Mia could tell by looking that they were all English tourists; they were all so pale, and there was a distinctly high proportion of men wearing socks with sandals.

'The airline desks are over there.'

Alex pointed and Mia followed his gaze. She nodded and started to walk in that direction. The desks were all open but didn't seem to be doing any business.

'Do you think I should ask if anyone has booked a ticket?' Mia said.

'Maybe,' Alex said, 'but it seems busy today. I am not sure that they would necessarily remember, and he would have arrived here last night.'

'What if he's not here? What if he's already left?' Mia said, feeling hopeless.

She couldn't bear the thought of having to go back and tell Tasha that Tim had gone home. A hand slipped in hers and gave it a squeeze. She looked down, even though she knew it was Alex. She would never admit it, but his touch was almost painfully comforting. It was a reminder of how good things had been, but also how they had gone so wrong. She allowed herself a moment of self-pity and then forced herself to focus on the task at hand. She needed to find Tim. There was too much hurt going around and if she could fix Tim and Tasha then who knew? Maybe there was hope for her and Alex too.

'If he has then it is not your fault, Mia.'

She looked up at him and saw regret in his eyes and she knew that he was feeling a sense of responsibility over what had happened. She would never admit it to anyone but a small part of herself was glad. She hadn't made her own mind up whether he was telling the truth about him and Tasha but the fact that he was acknowledging that he had played a part in the whole mess gave her a sense of hope. What she needed to do now was find Tim and get him and Tasha back together. Then maybe, just maybe, she and Alex would have a chance to figure out their own relationship.

16

Mia was running out of ideas of where to look and she was beginning to feel foolish. It seemed so unlikely now that she would be able to find Tim, let alone fix his relationship with Tasha.

'Perhaps we should check the restaurants. Maybe he's gone to get breakfast?'

Alex directed her through the crowds. The number of people seemed to have doubled in just a few minutes and Mia guessed that the passengers for the first flight out had arrived. Suddenly, she spotted a figure hunched over a coffee cup, right at the back of the small coffee express shop. She would recognise that sense of dejection anywhere! With a sense of reluctance, she released her hand from Alex's.

'I think you should wait here,' she said and weaved her way through the queue of people waiting to buy breakfast. She slipped quietly into the chair next to Tim, who was lost in his thoughts. Mia reached out and gently squeezed his arm.

'Hey, Tim,' she said, and Tim looked up slightly shocked.

He took a moment and then said, 'Is Tasha with you?'

'No,' Mia said, shaking her head. 'She finally cried herself to sleep a couple of hours ago.' Mia knew she was probably being unfair telling him this, but she also wanted Tim to know how badly Tasha was feeling.

'I guess getting caught out will do that to a person,' Tim said coldly.

'I think you know that's not why she is upset, Tim,' Mia said gently. After all, she had experienced similar feelings only recently, and so she knew how conflicted he felt.

'I don't know anything anymore,' he said morosely, before taking a sip of coffee.

'Why don't you come back with me and speak to her? Maybe you can sort this out.'

'I don't even know who she is anymore, Mia,' he said, but Mia felt a sense of relief that he looked so stricken. At least he was still feeling something.

'She's still Tasha, Tim. She loves you. I know that she does.'

He looked at her now and Mia could see that there were tears in his eyes. He and Tasha had been together since their teens. That was not something that was easy to walk away from, even if you felt like you had been betrayed.

'What's he doing here?' Tim's voice had changed and was now full of anger and outrage. It made Mia jump just a little, as it was so unlike him. She followed his gaze to Alex, who was standing at a distance watching.

'Alex is my friend, Tim, and he offered to drive me here to see if I could find you.'

'Feeling guilty for stealing another guy's fiancée, is he?'

Tim shifted in his seat and Mia wondered if he was going to leap up and face off with Adam again. She reached a hand out to settle him, forcing herself to speak calmly.

'Tim, I do know how you feel.'

'Do you?' he said, his voice raised to the point that the neighbouring table turned to stare at them.

'I do,' Mia said firmly. 'Alex and I are ... were together,' Mia said. The look on Tim's face told her she was not helping. 'What I mean,' she said quickly, 'is that I saw Alex and Tasha together and thought the same as you did, that there was something going on.'

Tim tore his eyes away from Alex and looked at her and she could see some sympathy in his face.

'I'm sorry, Mia,' he said. 'That's rough. Tasha betrayed you, too.' He looked even more stricken. She shook her head, this was not going like she hoped it would.

'No, what I mean is that I thought the same as you did, but I was wrong.'

Tim looked at her now a face full of sympathy and Mia knew what he was thinking, that she had been taken in by their lies too.

'They are just friends,' Mia said firmly, but wondered who she was trying to convince.

' 'Friends',' Tim said, making air quotes with his hands, 'don't behave like that.'

'Tim, they're friends. This is Greece, it's all a bit more ... overt here.' Mia knew that she was grasping at straws.

'I'm not sure what you're trying to say here. I mean, it sounds like you and him are over.' Tim jerked his head in Alex's direction. Mia grimaced.

'We haven't really had time to talk about things yet,' Mia said, and knew it sounded lame.

'Look, Mia, I know you're only trying to help here, but perhaps you need to focus on your relationship and leave Tasha to sort out her own mess for a change.'

He managed a smile and Mia knew she was looking at the Tim she had known for years. 'I mean that's why you came here isn't it? To escape from all the family drama that everyone expects you to sort out.' Now he reached over and squeezed her arm.

'I came here to write,' Mia said, and then laughed as Tim raised an eyebrow. 'Ok, I came here to escape for a little while.'

'And would I be right in guessing that you haven't got a whole lot done since the human whirlwind that is Tasha arrived?'

Mia shrugged and sighed.

'She's my little sister and I love her. I hate to see her like this.' She glanced to the side to read his reaction.

They sat in silence for a while and Mia watched him as he struggled with his emotions.

'I don't know what's going on with her. It just seemed to come out of nowhere.'

'So come and talk to her,' Mia said. 'Please? Just one conversation.'

Mia watched as Tim's eyes moved towards Alex.

'It doesn't look like I'm going to get a flight today, so at the very least I need to eat something that isn't airport food.'

Mia stood up and smiled in Alex's direction, since he was too far away to overhear their conversation.

'But I'm not going anywhere with him.' Tim's voice was steely and Mia knew there would be no convincing him to change his mind on that.

* * *

Mia took an anxious sip from her iced water and tried to think of something to say, thinking that life didn't get much more awkward than sitting between two childhood sweethearts who refused to speak and had spent the last half an hour glaring at each other. She tried to surreptitiously glance at her watch but Tasha spotted her and screwed up her face in a look of exasperation. That was it, she was done! Tim was right. Tasha needed to sort out her own mess. She needed to leave now or she was going to be late.

'Since all you two have done for the last half an hour is glare, I'm going to assume that my presence is not needed.'

Tasha opened her mouth to protest and her face was that of a five-year-old being left at the school gates for the first time.

'I'm late, I need to go.' She turned to Tim. 'You're welcome to crash at the apartment. Help yourself to anything you need.'

Mia picked up her bag and stepped away from the small table which was in the shade of the large, sun-bleached awning. She had one more thing to say and she knew if she didn't say it now, she never would.

'And, you two — you love each other, you always have. So just,' Mia waved her hands in frustration, 'sort it out, will you!'

She knew that the whole café was now staring at her and could feel the colour rising up her neck and so she walked away swiftly before the blush was in full bloom. She could tell without looking back that Tim and Tasha were staring at her. She wasn't usually the outburst type. In fact, she was usually the peacemaker, but not this time. She had come to Crete to make time to write and to give herself a break from the family drama. Tim was right; Tasha needed to sort herself out. She was a grown up after all.

★   ★   ★

All was quiet when Mia returned to the apartment and she wasn't sure if that was a good or a bad sign. She pushed her key into the lock and turned it, not wanting to step inside, not ready for the next slice of drama. The apartment was dark and silent. The curtains at the window moved in the slight breeze. In the dim light, Mia could make out two figures lying on top of the bed. Tim was holding Tasha in his arms; they looked like they had been talking and had just fallen asleep. The evening was a little cool and so Mia lifted the bedspread off the end of the bed and gently covered them with it.

She moved over to the chair by the window and sat down, feeling a mixture of relief that it seemed they had made up and a slight twinge of jealousy that it had been so much easier for them than it

174

seemed to be for her and Alex. Sitting in the dark, with no possibility of getting any sleep since Goldilocks and Co. were now in her bed, all Mia could do was think. How had things gone so badly with Alex? She knew that she had never felt this way before. She shook her head as the memories of their most recent arguments filled her head. What if she had been wrong about Alex and Tasha? It certainly seemed like she had, judging by the fact that Tim and Tasha seemed to have decided to at least try and move past it.

It wasn't just about Tasha though. Alex had come over all jealous when he knew that she was writing with Parker, who so far had been the perfect gentleman, not just to her but to all the other women on the course. Alex had been wrong about Parker, Mia was sure of it. Maybe, like Tasha and Tim, they just needed to talk it through. Without giving herself the chance to change her mind, she picked up her bag and headed back out the door.

17

Standing outside the taverna, Mia could hear someone moving around inside. The clink of glasses told her that someone was clearing up, although Mia could see no evidence of any late-night customers. She stepped onto the veranda and prayed that it would be Alex.

'Hello?' she called quietly, not wanting to make anyone jump at her sudden presence.

'Mia, my love! What a nice surprise,' Elizabeth said, putting down the cloth that she had been using to wipe the tables. 'Do you need some supper? I can fix you something.'

Mia smiled. 'No, thank you. I'm fine.' She wanted to say that she was looking for Alex, but somehow could not find the words.

Elizabeth pulled her into a hug and Mia hugged back, well used by now to being treated as if she were a long-lost daughter.

'Alessandro is in the kitchen, sweet girl,' Elizabeth said, whispering in her ear. Mia stood back from the hug and Elizabeth laughed. 'I know you well enough now, I think.'

Mia laughed too and the swing door to the kitchen was pushed open.

'Ma, are you laughing at your own jokes again?' Alex said, before his eyes fell on her. 'Mia,' he said, sounding surprised and, to Mia's ears, maybe even happy to see her. 'Is everything alright?' he asked, his face suddenly broken by a frown of concern.

'Yes,' Mia said with a smile, and for a moment she was struck by just how much help he had been to her over the months she had been in Crete. That alone should have meant she was at least prepared to listen to his side of the story.

'I just wanted to speak with you.' She made herself say the words out loud. Why were these situations so difficult? Why was it easier to stay angry and to hold on to the perceived hurt? Mia didn't know, but right now she knew what she needed to do — talk, and listen.

'We are nearly done here, my loves. Why not go sit out on the veranda? It is a lovely night and I will bring you some wine and meze.'

Mia held up her hands to protest. Elizabeth was working hard, and the last thing she wanted was for her to feel she had to wait on them.

'Tsh, Mia! You cannot have a serious conversation on an empty stomach, that is a recipe for disaster.' With that, Elizabeth bustled through to the kitchen.

'Best not to argue when a Greek mother has offered food,' Alex said with a smile. 'How is Natasha?' he asked.

'I haven't spoken to them. I left them at a café having a glaring contest, but when I got back from the villa, they were curled up together, asleep. So I'm assuming that's a good sign.'

Mia leaned forward and took a sip of her chilled wine before yielding to temptation and helping herself to a stuffed olive.

'It wasn't your fault, you know,' she said, willing herself to believe the words one hundred percent.

'I think that it was,' Alex said, looking away from her, seemingly suddenly interested in the town square. 'We may be in Greece, but Tasha is not from here and I should have been more careful.'

Mia nodded. Although these were the words she had wanted to hear, she suddenly felt as if she had taken a huge gulp of ice water and she knew what she needed to ask next. However painful it was, she needed to know.

'Do you have feelings for Tasha?'

Mia forced herself to look at him, to look him in the eye, ignoring her own feelings of embarrassment at being so forward.

'Of course not,' Alex said, his voice raised just a little. 'She is your sister and I like her. She is funny, and trying out her freedom, I think, but she is just a friend.'

Mia let the moments pass as she took

in this information and she knew she had a choice. She had to decide there and then whether she believed him or not. If she decided not to, then whatever they had would be over. No relationship could survive that kind of uncertainty, especially when it involved another family member who was always going to present in their lives.

'Ok then,' Mia said aloud, afraid that if she waited too long to speak, the doubts would come pouring back. She knew what she wanted. She wanted Alex back in her life. She wanted the opportunity to discover whether they were simply a holiday romance, or if there was something more. The thought surprised her, and her mind immediately went back to her plan. Falling in love had not been part of it, at least not the latest version. She had come here to write, the sensible part of her brain reminded her fiercely. But it had been so much easier to write, she had been so much more productive, knowing that Alex would be waiting for her when she finished. She pondered for a moment at her own motives. Was it really just about her writing? Was she selfishly using Alex for her own gain, like her own personal muse?

'You believe me?' Alex said softly, and Mia was brought back to the here and now.

Mia looked him in the eye. 'Yes,' she said firmly. 'I believe you.' Alex's face broke into a smile, and Mia realised she had missed that; she had missed him. She returned the smile and when Alex reached over to squeeze her hand, she returned that too.

'Then perhaps we can start over? How about I take you to dinner tomorrow night? Not here with the family, but maybe somewhere else, just the two of us.'

Mia smiled. There was nothing she would like more. In fact, the promise of dinner alone with Alex had seemed an impossible dream. Then she remembered — tomorrow was Saturday, and she had agreed to have dinner with Parker.

'Actually, tomorrow's not good for me,'

Mia said, focusing her eyes on her glass of wine.

'You have plans with your sister? I thought perhaps she would want to spend time with her fiancé.'

'Actually, Parker invited me out to dinner. We're going to talk about next week. Make sure that I'm prepared. He might even have a look at my novel.'

Mia's words came out in a rush and she knew she was over-explaining when she had no need to, but she couldn't seem to help it.

'Ok,' Alex said, and his voice was so even that Mia looked up, needing to check out his expression to see if she could tell what he was thinking. Alex just smiled, but Mia wondered if she could see a little tightness around his eyes, like he was making an effort to hold his tongue.

'We're just friends, you know,' Mia blurted out, again not sure why she was explaining herself. Somehow she felt she had to reassure Alex, which under the recent circumstances seemed ridiculous. 'It's no big deal.'

Alex shrugged and Mia felt herself getting a little annoyed.

'What?' she said, and it came out sharply.

'Nothing, Mia,' Alex said, and held his hands up as if admitting defeat. 'I have told you what I think of this man before, there is no need to go over old ground, I think, and you are an adult and can make up your own mind.'

Mia took a sip of wine to give her a few moments to try and work out how she felt about his response. Part of her felt annoyed that somehow he was making a point but the other part of her thought she should just accept it at face value. If not, the evening, which had showed some real promise for their relationship, could deteriorate into another fight. A fight over something that was not worth fighting over. Alex didn't like Parker, but Mia had always found him to be the perfect gentleman and she had no concerns that the dinner was anything more than just dinner, between friends.

'Good,' Mia said. 'How about Sunday?

Or would you rather spend it with your family?'

Alex smiled. 'I have dinner with them every night, Mia. They will understand, I am sure.'

Mia couldn't help but smile back. Perhaps everything was really falling back into place after all the events of the last few weeks. Then she noticed Alex glance at his watch.

'Is it late?' she asked, realising that she had left her own watch on her desk in the apartment, which was very unlike her — she had an almost pathological need to always know what the time was, but then, that was what happened when you planned your life like she did. Alex nodded.

'Yes, even by Greek standards. Alas, I must get some rest or I will be sleeping at the wheel when I collect from the airport in … three hours.'

'Three hours? Eek! I'm so sorry, Alex, you get off to bed and I'll clear up.' Mia felt herself blush a little and so busied herself collecting up plates.

'Ma would never let me hear the end of it,' he said, reaching out for a plate just as Mia did. Their hands touched and Mia felt a jolt run through her. She had been so careful not to be physically too near Alex since the issue over Tasha, and his touch reminded her why. She wasn't sure if Alex felt it too, but Mia didn't have time to wonder about it as she watched the plate fall from her hand. It slid off the table and crashed to the ground, shattering into tiny pieces. Mia immediately dropped to her knees to start clearing up, feeling embarrassed that she had been so careless.

'Careful, Mia. It is just a plate. It's not worth hurting yourself over.'

A strong hand reached for her arm and pulled her back. Mia could feel that Alex was now kneeling beside her, and her breath caught in her throat at his nearness. Since Alex had not let go of her arm, she knew that she needed to look at him, and she did. The sight of him made her heart flip. His look of concern mixed with amusement at her actions reminded her of the time he had rescued her from the terrible accommodation she had so carefully booked. Her breath rushed out as he carefully brushed her hair away from her face. She blinked and he moved closer. Mia was expecting him to kiss her but he seemed uncertain. Reaching up gently she pulled his face to hers and tentatively brushed her lips to his, as she had done the first time they kissed. She watched his face carefully to check that she had read the signals right. The lights dancing in his eyes told her that the spell had not been broken.

Now, Alex pulled her into him and she found herself cradled in his arms. She felt like she was where she belonged and wanted the moment to last for ever, but the sensible part of her brain reminded her of the time. She sighed and pulled away slowly. Alex's eyebrows shaped the question that he hadn't asked.

'The time,' Mia said softly. 'You need to get some sleep, remember?'

Alex kissed her again. 'Sleep is over-rated,' he whispered, holding her close to his chest.

Mia closed her eyes and willed herself to just relax and be in the moment, but the nagging sensation would not be ignored. This was one of the downsides of being a planner whose life was dictated by the ticking clock. This time she used the palms of her hands to create some distance. She knew she would fall straight back into kissing Alex if she was too close. Alex sighed and leaned back, taking his weight on his arms. He tilted his head to one side and Mia smiled.

'You need rest. I won't have you falling asleep at the wheel on my account.'

Alex leaned in for another kiss but Mia put her hand out to stop him. She couldn't help but laugh.

'Stop, Alex. There will be plenty of time to kiss tomorrow.'

'It is tomorrow,' Alex said, and Mia loved that she could see his eyes dancing, mirroring her own happiness.

Reluctantly she forced herself to stand up. Alex puffed out some air and looked for all the world as if he were sulking.

Mia shook her head but couldn't keep a straight face. With a giggle she held out her hand and hauled him to his feet. She tried to take a step away but found herself pulled into his arms. Her head nestled underneath his chin and again she felt lost in the moment. This is it, she told herself, this is happiness and love. The last thought caught her almost unaware. But, as many of her friends had told her before, you will know real love when you feel it — and she did.

'I love you, Alex,' she whispered, not even sure if she had said it loud enough for him to hear.

'S'agapo, Mia,' Alex whispered back, before kissing her gently on the head.

18

Mia stood in the shower and let the water wash over her head, hoping it would block out the noise from the rest of the apartment. Tasha's voice was raised, verging on hysterical and if the last twenty-four years had taught Mia anything, she knew what that meant. Tasha was about to lose it, big time.

Since Tim had returned, Mia had done her best to stay out of their relationship, taking on board the advice that it was time Tasha learnt to fix her own problems. But the crashing sound made Mia's mind up for her. Something had obviously been broken and since none of the contents of the apartment actually belonged to her, that was the final straw. She grabbed her towel, wrapped it round herself and stomped out of the tiny alcove that was the bathroom.

'Stop it,' Mia said, as she watched

189

Tasha reach for the next thing that she was clearly about to throw in Tim's direction. The tone Mia used left no room for argument. After all, she had years of experience of dealing with her sister's tantrums. She had learnt that yelling didn't get you very far. Tasha was frozen in place, arm in the air with another of the heavy pottery coffee cups in her outstretched hand.

'Put that down,' Mia said, crossing her arms and raising a cool eyebrow. 'Now.'

Tasha looked at her hand as if she had just realised the cup was in it, and slowly put it back down on the table. Tim stood with fists tightly clenched by his sides.

'I don't know what's got into her,' he said, and it was clear to Mia he was having to work hard to keep his temper in check. Mia wondered for a moment what had happened to the two lovebirds who had, prior to Tasha's trip to Crete, never exchanged a cross word.

Mia held up a hand to stop Tim from talking.

'I really, really don't want to know,'

Mia said. 'I'm having a hard time working out what's worse — the glaring and sullen silences, or the yelling and throwing things.'

She turned her attention to Tasha.

'And you are going to replace that,' Mia said, gesturing at the shattered cup. 'It's not even yours. And regardless, what makes you think it's ever ok to throw something at another person's head?'

Mia knew she was losing her temper, something she always worked hard not to do, but she'd had enough. This was supposed to be her time, and although she was deeply grateful Tasha had arrived safely, Mia was resentful that she had brought all the drama from home to her retreat.

'Seriously, you two. I'm done. I'm not a relationship counsellor! You two need to figure this out and stop behaving like stroppy teenagers!'

Mia took a deep breath. She had been thinking about this for a while, wondering if it was the right thing to do. She wondered if it would be the thing that made

Tasha and Tim sort themselves out.

'You need to find a place to stay that's not here,' Mia said quickly, before she chickened out. 'I can't take this. I worked so hard to save the money I needed to take six months out, to spend some time on me for a change. I love you both,' she looked from Tasha to Tim, 'but you need to leave. You need to go somewhere you can figure this out.'

Tasha just stared and Tim looked at his flip-flops.

'I mean it, Tash. I can't figure this out for you. You have to decide what you want; both of you do.'

For the first time, Mia understood the expression 'the silence was deafening'. She sighed, scooped up the underwear and light cotton dress she had draped over one of the chairs and walked back into the bathroom. She knew that if she stood there any longer she would default back into big sister mode and try to fix whatever it was that was going on between them. It wasn't easy to get dressed in the tiny cubicle but she had got it down to an art form. She looked at herself in the mirror and told herself silently that she had done the right thing. Looking down at her hands, she realised that she had crossed her fingers. Tilting her head to one side she listened carefully. It had gone quiet, but Mia wasn't sure that was necessarily a good sign. Perhaps they had gone back to glaring at each other.

The minutes ticked by and Mia knew that she couldn't hide in the tiny bathroom for much longer. For one thing, it was hot and she didn't want to turn up to dinner all sweaty, and for another, this was her apartment and she was done tiptoeing around it.

The reason for the quietness became quickly apparent. Even Tasha couldn't argue by herself. She was curled up on the bed, hugging a cushion and Mia held in a sigh. It wasn't that she didn't feel sorry for Tash, it was just that she was tired of trying to fix everything for her.

'Tash, I have to go or I'll be late for dinner, even by Greek standards.'

Mia knew that she probably sounded

uncaring to Tasha's ears but to say anything remotely sympathetic would mean that she would have to stay.

'Tash?'

'I'm fine, you go.' In a voice that sounded anything but.

'You could come. There's always room at Elizabeth's table and you need to eat something.'

'I'm not hungry.' The reply was muffled as Tasha had her head buried in a pillow.

'I love you, Tasha, you know that, right?' Mia felt a mix of emotions — partly annoyance that despite her best intentions she was late, and partly concern for her little sister.

'I know, I love you too.'

'I really think you and Tim need to sort this out, between you.' Mia was feeling desperate now. She knew she wouldn't be able to walk out unless there was some sign from Tasha, that she was actually ok.

Mia risked a glance at her watch.

'I'm fine, really. And you wouldn't want

to be late.' Tasha's voice had gone back to sullen and Mia could feel her frustration and anger building again.

'Ok,' Mia said, and took a few steps towards the door, her hand on the latch. She couldn't quite bring herself to step through.

'Mia!' Now it seemed it was Tasha's turn to sound exasperated. 'I can't sort out my life if you're hovering over me all the time!'

A few days before, Mia would have welcomed Tasha saying those words but in that moment she almost felt as if Tasha had slapped her across the face. Not trusting herself to turn around or to answer she opened the door and headed down the stairs.

★   ★   ★

When Mia arrived back at her apartment, she wasn't sure what she would find. She wasn't sure what she wanted to find. Tasha still there or Tasha gone seemed equally troubling prospects. Opening the door, all was quiet and her eyes strayed to her comprehensive plan that was stuck to the wall. So much had happened in the last few months that she hadn't planned for. Although it was unexpected, most of it was good. Maybe planning wasn't always the answer. She laughed out loud at herself. That was one thing she never thought she'd say.

She noticed a handwritten note on the small table, leaning against a vase containing a single flower. She needed to find out what Tasha had to say.

Mia picked up the note.

Dear Mia

Tim and I have talked and we have found a place to stay. He has one more week of holiday and we are going to try and work it out. I know that you are pretty fed up with me right now but if you want to see me then Alex knows where we are. Hope to see you soon.

Love Tash x

Mia put the letter down, walked across to

the window and tried to sort through her feelings. There was the all-too-familiar twinge of guilt even though her brain was telling her she had done the right thing. Tasha was an adult and she needed to sort out her own problems. For too long her family had relied upon her to fix every little problem, to be the negotiator, and maybe she had been too quick to step in, maybe she was part of the problem. Mia walked over and clicked on the kettle. What she needed was a cup of tea. It was always easier to blame other people, to focus on what they had done rather than your own part in it.

She reached for her mobile phone and sent a text to Alex. She hated to admit it but she needed to know where Tasha was, to check that it was safe. She knew she was being ridiculous, Tasha wasn't a child and Tim would never let anything bad happen to her. She waited for the tell-tale beep.

'Staying somewhere safe, Mia. Do not worry!'

Mia smiled at the thought that he knew

her well enough to read between the lines of her text. There was another beep.

'I miss you.'

'I miss you too,' Mia texted back and then hugged her phone to her chest. Was it possible that life could work out like this, unexpected and unplanned? She grinned to herself; it seemed so.

'See you tomorrow?'

'Of course ... but only if you finish your word count.'

Mia couldn't help the grin that was spreading across her face. Alex could not be more perfect. Not only was he incredibly handsome and kind but he understood her. Not only did he understand her dreams but he did everything he could to support her achieving them. There was only one word to describe Alex, she thought as she curled up in bed, her apartment back to its calm and peaceful self. He was perfect. Apart from the Parker thing. The thought made her frown and so she brushed it aside. Nobody was perfect, of course, and if the worst side of Alex was that he could be a little jealous, she was sure she could live with that.

19

By the time Saturday came round, Mia was finding it hard to contain her excitement. Parker was taking her out to dinner and they were going to discuss her novel. What was even more exciting was that Parker had hinted that someone, a publisher someone, wanted to read her novel. Although she was afraid to let her 'baby' out there, she also knew that any advice from Parker would be hugely valuable. The only thing that dulled the edges of her excitement was that Alex had not shared in it. Mia had always thought that having a boyfriend who could be a bit jealous would be exciting, but actually it was kind of tedious. Alex had been so sombre over lunch today that Mia had almost convinced herself that he was going to break the relationship off. All thoughts of that went out her mind when he kissed her goodbye. That was not the way you kissed someone if you were about to dump them, of that much Mia was sure!

She showered and changed into a black cotton dress, one that reached her ankles in deference to the fact that she was not having a romantic dinner with her boyfriend but instead was attending a working dinner in which she wanted to impress a writer she admired. She was just checking that she had her precious notebook with her one more time when a car horn sounded in the street below. A quick peek through the thin curtains told her that it was Parker. She recognised his old, beaten up Fiat instantly. Allowing herself one last check on her notebook which, unless it had grown legs in the last two hours, remained firmly in her bag, she let herself out of the apartment.

The taverna was further along the coast, a place that Parker said was unknown to all but the most brave explorers, where the food was outstanding. Mia secretly thought it would be hard to beat Elizabeth's cooking but kept that to herself. She didn't want to start the evening off on a bad note when he had kindly offered to help her with her novel. The car wound its way round narrow lanes that were little more than paths, and Mia began to wonder if they would ever get there. Then, seemingly out of the blue, Mia saw a series of lights, no more than small pin pricks.

As they drove closer, Mia could make out a string of pale yellow fairy lights that had been haphazardly strung across the edge of the roof of the taverna. It looked more like a shack to Mia's eyes, as it had areas that had clearly been patched with corrugated iron, but the wide veranda was full of people eating and drinking, and she took that as a good sign. The only voices she could hear were Greek and there were large family groups of all ages. Clearly this was a place to meet friends and family. Mia felt suddenly as if she should not be there, as if she was intruding on something private, but Parker opened the car door and offered her his hand. Not knowing what else to do, she took it and allowed herself to be pulled along to the gap in the veranda fence that served as the entrance to the taverna.

'Parker!' a voice sounded, with a heavy accent. 'You are come at last.'

The older man was tanned and wrinkled. He held his arms open wide and, as expected, Parker stepped into them and allowed both of his cheeks to be kissed. The man rattled off a question in Greek and Parker turned to Mia.

'Kristos, this Mia, my friend who also writes,' Parker said, and Mia was treated to the same greeting. Having been in Crete for a few months she didn't resist; she was used to strangers treating her like long-lost family. She was released and then found herself guided to a table for two set out on the other side of the tavern. It had amazing views of the ocean and Mia gasped in surprise.

'I told you you'd love it,' Parker said. 'Not only is it an amazing view, which is good for the creative juices, but the food is to die for.'

There were no menus and so Mia let Parker order the food. She had no idea what they were getting, but had yet to find anything Greek that she didn't enjoy, so she settled back in the chair and allowed her gaze to wander over the horizon, where the sun was an orange half circle, moving so fast that she knew it would soon disappear.

Twenty minutes later, with full wine glasses and a selection of meze that Mia had to admit were very good, she wondered when they would get down to talking about writing. So far they had touched on a little of the Tasha-related drama and Parker had told her about his own family back in the States. Whilst this was interesting, Mia had to do her best not to fidget.

'Well, perhaps now is the time to get to business,' Parker said, placing one last olive in his mouth. Mia could feel herself blush, as if all her efforts to appear casual and relaxed had been seen through. Parker merely laughed.

'I take it you have your notebook with

you?' he asked with a mischievous air.

'A good writer is never without their notebook,' Mia replied, smiling.

'Indeed, but most writers carry a notebook for making notes. I know very few writers who keep all of their precious work on paper these days.' Parker raised an eyebrow, and since they had had this conversation several times before, Mia simply raised an eyebrow back.

'I've told you before. It's the way I write. I can't type my stories. I have to feel the pen and the paper. It's the only way it works for me.' Mia took a sip of her wine, and waited.

'That I understand, but why not type it up once you have written it in your notebook?' He gestured at the tatty, beaten up Moleskine that Mia had placed on the table but kept a protective hand on.

'Because,' she said with an exaggerated eye roll — they had also had this conversation before — 'I edit it in paper form too. I only type it up once I'm happy with it. I tried it your way, but I lost the thread, the heart of the story.' Mia frowned a little at the memory. 'Anyway I thought you said that all the best writers have their funny little ways.'

Parker raised his glass in mock salute which told her she had yet again won the argument, or at least they had reached a truce.

'So, can I see it?' he asked casually, as if he knew how much she was dying for him to read it.

Mia drummed her fingers on her precious notebook. She had always known it would be hard to hand over but now it felt like she was giving away part of herself. Forcing herself to take a deep breath, she slid the notebook over to him and with an effort removed her hand. Parker gave her a look which suggested he understood her dilemma, but Mia had a sudden urge to be away from him. She stood up abruptly.

'I think I'll just go and powder my nose,' she said, wincing as she used such a ridiculously outdated phrase. Parker simply nodded, all his attention fixed on the first page of her novel.

In the small toilet that served as the ladies, Mia splashed a little cold water on her face and, looking in the mirror, told herself firmly to get a grip. This was what it was all about, this was what coming to Crete had been all about. It hadn't been part of the plan, of course. She'd been going to finish her book, polish it and then when she got home, start to send it out to publishers. But if Crete and Alex had taught her anything, it was that the best things in life could rarely be planned for. Allowing herself one more deep breath she headed back out to Parker. He had remained engrossed and Mia allowed herself to feel that this was a good sign. She took her seat and watched as the lights from a car lit up the now-darkened view. The lights seemed to move all over the place as if someone was driving way too fast for the uneven road surface.

Mia watched as the car screeched up, into a tiny gap between two other parked cars. She held her breath, expecting to hear the sound of metal grinding against metal, but there was nothing other than the wave of sand and stones left in its wake. Her attention was drawn back to Parker, who let out a little chuckle. Mia studied his face in the candlelight, trying to make out if that was a good chuckle or a patronising one, like she had fallen into one of the many traps that new writers could find themselves in. His eyes didn't stray from the page and when he turned it, it was as if he couldn't wait to read more. Or maybe her imagination was playing out the scene she had always dreamt of when she finally allowed someone else to read her work in its entirety.

Mia heard raised Greek voices, urgent, not just loud and relaxed. She tore her eyes away from Parker and realised that Kristos was weaving his way between the other tables behind them. She frowned as she caught a glimpse of the person in his wake who was making his way determinedly towards them, despite their host's protests. Kristos said something in Greek to Parker who murmured and waved him away, refusing to be distracted.

'Mia!' came a familiar voice.

Mia nearly fell off her chair.

'Alex! What are you doing here?'

Now that Alex's face was bathed in the light of both candles and fairy lights Mia could see his expression and she felt as if her heart had stopped.

20

'What is it? What's the matter?' she asked, barely able to get the words out. Alex's face was so grave that she knew something was terribly wrong.

'Is it Tasha?' she asked, her voice barely a whisper as her mind raced to think of all the things that could have befallen her little sister. Alex shook his head and it looked to Mia as if he was struggling to find the words to tell her the most terrible news.

'Alex, please,' she said, reaching out for his hand. She was dimly aware that Parker had stopped reading and was watching them closely.

'Is it my parents, your parents?'

Alex cut her off with a raised hand.

'No, Mia. Everyone is well. I did not mean to scare you.' He stopped and she could see agony in his eyes.

'Then what is it?'

She still felt concern but there was now a tinge of something else. Did he not trust her? With Parker? They had spoken about this at length and she thought he had understood her. Now she felt anger start to grow and more than a little embarrassment as she wondered if Parker had guessed what was going on.

'This man cannot be trusted,' Alex said, so formally that in any other circumstances Mia might have laughed. But she was not laughing now. She carefully wiped her mouth on her napkin, lay it on the table and turned to Parker.

'Please excuse us, I will only be a minute.'

Parker nodded and Mia couldn't tell if he were amused or annoyed. That was something she would have to find out later. She stood primly and indicated with her arm that Alex should lead the way out of the taverna. Her face left nothing to the imagination; she was furious, and she showed it. Mia made her way stiffly down the veranda steps, aware that many in the taverna were glancing at them curiously.

The only good thing was that they were about to argue in English, and she hoped that the other diners would not be able to understand all of what was about to happen.

Alex turned and looked at her, his face unreadable.

'What do you think you are doing?' Mia said, managing to keep her voice low but having to force the words out between clenched teeth. 'We talked about this. There is nothing going on between me and Parker. He is simply providing me some feedback on my novel. I thought you understood that.'

'That is not what he is doing, Mia,' Alex said softly, and Mia had a flashback to their very first argument, which somehow that made her madder. He always seemed to be able to take the moral high ground, always believed that he was right.

'You may not trust Parker, but I thought you trusted me,' Mia said, deciding to take another track.

Alex reached out for her hand.

'Of course I trust you, Mia. That is not what this is about.'

Mia freed her hand from his. She couldn't concentrate with him so close and she needed to think clearly.

'Alex, I used to think your jealousy was kind of endearing, but this is ridiculous! You have thoroughly embarrassed me in front of Parker — the man who may well play a crucial part in me achieving my dream. A dream I thought you understood.' Mia felt tears build as she felt that once again, no one really understood how important her writing was to her.

'I am not jealous, Mia. Not of that man.' He used the word 'man' with such disdain that Mia took a step back. She was feeling exasperated and for the first time ever, she wanted Alex to leave her alone. That thought brought real pain but was nothing compared to the realisation that perhaps she didn't know him at all. That he was nothing like the man she had believed him to be.

'Mia, please.' Alex's eyes were alight now. 'Please give me a few minutes to explain. Then I will leave if you wish me to.'

Mia felt once again that perhaps he could read her thoughts but she was too angry and confused to care in that moment.

'Fine,' she said, crossing her arms. She would give him that.

'Tasha ... ' Alex started, and the fear was back.

'What about her?' Mia failed to keep the alarm from her voice.

'Tasha wanted to come and speak to you about this, but she was worried that you would not want to see her, would not want to listen to what she had to say. So I promised her that I would come to you.' Alex couldn't stand still and paced away from her before turning back.

'I don't understand,' Mia said, shaking her head at the thought that Tasha felt she couldn't speak to her about something. 'Is it about Tim?'

'I can see that you are in a hurry so I will make my story quick.' Mia felt that sting. 'Tasha was out in the town. She was having some time apart from Tim and so she went to a café. There was a man there, talking on his mobile phone, loudly, with an American accent.'

Mia shook her head. She had no idea where this was going but she wanted to get back to Parker and her book.

'Tasha thought nothing of it until he started to read out something from his laptop. Then she knew that something was wrong. She had heard the words before, the story.'

Alex paused and Mia wondered if it was for effect or if he were merely checking he had her attention.

'Those words, the story he was reading. They were yours.'

Mia let out a tight laugh. That was impossible. She had no idea how Alex had convinced Tasha to take part in this little ruse but it was over. She held up her hands.

'Do you expect me to believe that Alex? Really?'

Alex reached for her again but she twisted away.

'It is the truth, Mia. Tasha stayed and listened, they were your words. He was reading them out to someone over the phone. Tasha was sure that he was talking to someone in America.'

Mia shook her head fiercely.

'She must be mistaken. He couldn't have my story. Today is the first time he's even seen it.'

'But you told me that you have read parts at the writing group.'

'Well, yes, but how ... '

'Where is your story now, Mia?' Alex said softly.

'Parker is reading it. But none of this makes sense, Alex. You must see how crazy this sounds.'

'Then let us confront him. Ask him, then you will know,' Alex said, simply.

'I can't confront him! I would be accusing him of the worst thing a writer could do. I don't believe it, I can't. If I accuse him, he will never help me.' Mia could feel panic rising inside her.

'If you don't, you might lose your story. If Tasha is right, he has stolen it, stolen part of you.'

Mia looked up sharply, wondering if Alex was playing some kind of game. But there was such pain in his eyes that she wanted to reach out for him, to hold him and be held by him. Her mind raced. Why would he make this up? What could he hope to gain by making up such a tale? He must have known it would make her angry. Maybe even cause her to break up with him. A cold, dull ache settled in her stomach as she allowed herself to consider if Alex was telling the truth. She looked at him again and felt the fear, not at losing someone she loved but at losing the thing she loved. The work that she had invested so much of herself in. She spun on her heel and dashed back into the taverna. She didn't need to look to know that Alex was right there with her.

The sound of a mobile phone camera taking a photo told her everything she needed to know in that moment. Parker was sat at the table, her notebook held open by one of his splayed hands, his mobile in the other — and then the tell-tale flash as another photo was taken. Parker looked up then and dropped his phone back on the table.

'What are you doing?' Mia managed to say, although she felt like she would never be able to speak again.

'Just checking my phone for messages. This is good, Mia, really good,' Parker said calmly, as he gestured to her note-book. 'It needs some work, but I think if we can get you together with a really good editor, you have a real shot at getting published.'

Mia marvelled at the bare-faced lie she had just been told. Her instinct told her that he was lying but everything about him seemed so genuine.

'You were taking a photo,' she said.

Parker laughed. 'You know me and technology. I probably did. I have trouble working out which button to press to read my messages.'

His eyes glanced innocently from Mia to Alex.

'Everything alright?'

Alex made to take a step forward but

Mia put out a hand to stop him. She needed to find out the truth, whatever it was, and she was going to be the one to do it.

'Were you taking photos of my notebook?' she asked, scanning his face for any signs of deception, although she knew she wouldn't be able to see any. Parker, it seemed, was a consummate liar.

Parker looked confused. 'Why would I want to do that? I told you, Mia, I have trouble with my phone.'

Mia wondered if she detected a slight twitch when he said those last words.

'Let me see.' She held out her hand expectantly.

'Mia, I'm not giving you my phone. It's private. I'm surprised you would even ask such a thing!' He sound indignant now but Mia would not be put off.

'I think you have been taking images of my manuscript.'

Parker took a sip of wine.

'Now, Mia, why would I want to do something like that?' There was a hint of danger in his voice now, Mia was sure of it.

'To pass it off as your own!' The words came from behind Mia's shoulder. Alex was clearly fighting to keep his temper in check. One glance told Mia that she had never seen Alex so angry.

'I've no idea what your boyfriend has been telling you, Mia. But we were having a pleasant business meeting to discuss how best to present your book to a publisher. I would have thought that was more important to you than any game you are currently playing with him.' Parker's tone was so dismissive that Mia was now certain.

'Someone heard you, you know,' Mia said quietly.

'Heard me what?'

'Reading my story over the phone to someone, a publisher, maybe your agent?'

'Mia, this is ridiculous. Tonight is the first time I've seen your story. When would I have had the chance to do this?' He took another sip of his wine and looked at her with a raised eyebrow.

'But it's not the first time that you've heard it, is it?'

Parker looked as if he was about to laugh it off so Mia continued before she lost her nerve.

'I wondered why you were encouraging me to read out my work every night, when others didn't have the chance. Is that how you got it? Is that how you got my novel? But you didn't have all of it. I never read the last few chapters and you needed those. So that's why you invited me here. You just needed an opportunity to get the rest of it.'

21

Mia felt breathless and unsteady on her feet as the full weight of what was happening hit her. She felt Alex put a steadying hand on her shoulder. His presence was so comforting and gave her the strength she needed to finish what she had started. Parker merely gazed at her.

'And how do you plan to prove it, Mia?' he said, all pretence gone now. She felt for the first time she was seeing the real Parker, hard, cold and self-assured.

Mia reached out and snatched her notebook back.

'With this,' she said, waving it at him.

'Mia, who do you think the publishing world will believe? You, a wannabe writer with no publishing history? Or me, an established author with a body of work?'

Mia could feel herself start to shake with anger and frustration.

'I won't let you get away with this,' she

said, holding back tears.

'There's nothing to get away with. My editor has all but the last few chapters, which I will type up and send tonight.' He lifted up his phone and waved it at her before standing.

'There is nothing you can do, except perhaps start again. You have real talent, Mia. I have a feeling that my new book will be on the *New York Times* bestseller list. You might want to keep an eye out for it.'

Parker stood and made to walk past them. Alex grabbed at his arm. Parker looked at him, unconcerned.

'I wouldn't do that, if I were you. It won't help your little girlfriend if you end up in some Greek prison, now, will it? I suspect she is having a bad enough day as it is.'

Parker smiled unsympathetically at Mia, who reached out an arm for Alex and pulled him away. Alex looked torn, like he could barely contain himself, but when he saw her face, he let go of Parker and watched him pay the bill and leave.

'Mia, I am so, so sorry,' he said, and pulled her into his arms, and let her cry.

★ ★ ★

It had been over a week since Mia's fateful meeting with Parker and she hadn't written a word. She had barely spoken a word either. She knew her friends and family were concerned but she just couldn't think of anything to say. Tasha and Alex visited everyday but there was nothing that they could do to break her mood. The truth was that she had nobody to blame but herself. She hadn't listened to Alex when he had tried to tell her of Parker's reputation, which, as it turned out, was not that he was a ladies' man, but that he was considered to be untrustworthy.

Mia had been staring at the wall for over an hour. Her cup of tea sat, untouched, on the small table. Her plan, which was so detailed and written by someone so sure that you could plan for everything, seemed to mock her. She stood up suddenly. The full cup of cold tea slopped all over the table and started to run onto the floor. Mia ignored it. She knew what she needed to do. She marched across the room and grabbed at one corner of the large piece of paper that was her plan and pulled. It ripped jaggedly, with each piece of paper tearing away from the whole. For the first time in three days she felt a sense of satisfaction.

'Mia! What are you doing?' Alex stepped through the front door that Mia had stopped bothering to lock, since it meant she had to get up and answer it, and grabbed hold of her hand which was poised to tear off another strip.

'It's worthless. I'm getting rid of it. I can't stare at it anymore.'

Mia didn't trust herself not to cry so kept her gaze firmly fixed on the latest tear in the paper, which had ripped her goal of 'send to first on list of agents' in half. Her mind seemed to register the irony.

'Stop, please, Mia. You are bleeding.'

Mia glanced down and saw that the paper had caused a shallow but long cut along her index finger and it was bleeding freely. She frowned. It seemed like even physical pain wasn't registering at the moment. She allowed Alex to gently guide her back to the chair and sit her down. He knelt down before her, reached for a tissue and dabbed at her finger.

'Mia, you can't go on like this. I am worried about you, as is Tasha, not to mention Ma, who is threatening to come over and force feed you.'

His smile was so gentle and warm that Mia knew she was going to cry. Somehow, knowing that people cared only made her feel worse and she couldn't ignore the nagging feeling of guilt of what she knew she was putting them through.

'I'm sorry,' she whispered and then the tears started. Mia had cried so much over the last few days that she wondered if she would ever be able to stop.

Alex lifted her easily in his arms and walked them over to the small sofa. He sat down with Mia on his lap and held her, rubbing her back and letting her cry. After what felt like an age, the tears started to slow and her breathing settled. She snuggled into Alex, tucking her head under his chin and he leaned down and kissed her.

'Now, you will come to dinner, I think?' he said softly.

Mia shook her head like a child who didn't want to do something.

'I can't, Alex, look at me. I'm a mess!'

Mia indicated her pyjamas and her hair which she hadn't washed since it had all happened. She was suddenly acutely aware that she probably didn't smell great either. She wriggled so that she could put some distance between her and Alex but he held her tight.

'I do not care and neither will Ma. If you don't come to her tonight then she will come to you and she will be fierce.'

Mia could feel his smile.

'And besides you have time,' he said, glancing at his watch.

'I'm not sure I can face them, Alex. I feel like such an idiot and I'll most likely cry. It will be embarrassing.'

'Mia, you are in Greece now. We do not

hold back our emotions as you English do. You will come and have dinner with the people who love you and want to take care of you. They will not mind how you look or behave.'

He leaned his head back so he could look at her.

'But they might mind a little how you smell, my love.'

Mia saw the twinkle in his eye and knew he was teasing but she elbowed him in the ribs just to be sure. With a sigh, she untangled herself from him and headed towards the shower.

'You'll wait for me?'

Alex shook his head at her ridiculous question. 'But of course, Mia. Where else would I be?'

Mia knew she was hanging back, not quite ready to face her family, for that is how she saw them these days. Alex was waiting patiently for her but with a smile on his face.

'I suspect Elizabeth has made them wait for you Mia, so perhaps we should go in before they get too hungry.'

He leaned in and kissed her gently and somehow it gave Mia courage.

The usual noise of the family didn't lessen but greetings were thrown in her direction and Mia felt like it was going to be ok. No one seemed to be treating her any differently but they were pleased to see her, as always. Elizabeth appeared from the kitchen with two trays laden with meze which she placed carefully on the table, before pulling Mia in to a quick, tight hug.

'I've been worried about you, lovely girl.'

Mia smiled as she pulled away and it was genuine. For the first time she felt like perhaps life would go on after all. There was the scrape of a chair and then Tasha was flinging her arms around her. All bad feeling and hurt from their last meeting was forgotten.

'I'm so glad you came, Mia. We have missed you and I've been so worried.' Tasha held Mia's face in her hands. 'I'm so sorry,' she said, and Mia could see that she was about to cry, and knew that if she did, her own tears would fall.

'It's not your fault Tasha, you did everything you could. I was naive and stupid.' She could feel herself start to tremble as the full force of emotions started to build again.

'Perhaps we should sit?' Alex said, directing them to two chairs at the end of the table.

Mia nodded and smiled greetings to the extended family and did a double take when she saw Tim, deep in discussion with one of Alex's uncles. She looked at Tasha questioningly.

'We're good,' she said with a smile. 'I mean, we have some things we need to work out, but we know that we want to, which is something at least.'

Mia knew that look. Tasha was seeking her approval. She reached over and squeezed her hand.

'I couldn't be happier, Tash. You two are meant for each other.'

Mia smiled as some of the tension in Tasha's shoulders seemed to melt away.

'I don't think we're the only ones.'

Mia followed Tasha's eyes to where

Alex was helping Elizabeth sort out drinks to go with dinner.

'Who'd have thought it?' Mia said. 'That wasn't part of the plan.'

'Well, I've said to you many times before, you can't plan for everything,' Tasha said sagely, as if she were the older sister, and they both laughed.

'It is good to see you laugh, Mia,' Alex said, as he handed her a cold glass of her favourite wine.

Mia took a deep breath.

'I'm sorry I've been such a drama queen, it just … '

'You don't need to explain to us, we understand. Really we do,' Tasha said quickly. 'I know how much of your life you have invested in your book and this whole situation is so unfair.'

Mia took a sip of her wine to try and steady her thoughts. She knew she needed to let go. There was nothing to be done and moping about it was certainly not helping.

'What's done is done, Tash. I know I need to move on but I guess I just need a little time to figure out what I'm going to do next.'

Tasha wriggled in her seat and if Mia didn't know better, she would say her sister was both excited and nervous.

'But it's not done,' she said with a little squeal. Mia just stared and Alex looked amused.

'I don't understand,' Mia said flatly, not letting the seed of hope at Tasha's words be planted.

'Well, I've been giving it some thought. How did Parker get your manuscript? It was when you were at the retreat, right?'

Mia shrugged.

'And he runs these retreats a lot, doesn't he?'

'Yes, but I don't see how that helps,' Mia said, fighting back a wave of misery. How had she been so foolish?

'Well, I took it one step forward. I wondered — what if Parker had done this to someone else?' Tasha said, eagerly.

'I'm sure he has,' Mia said, sadly, 'but again, that doesn't change anything.'

'Ah, but it does,' Tasha said, practically bouncing in her seat.

Mia took a deep breath. She was tired and emotional and that was not good for her temper.

'All it tells us is that I wasn't the only person in the world to fall for his tricks.'

Tasha shook her head.

'It's more than that, if you happen to have found those other people.' Tasha's eyes were bright and Mia knew that she must be missing something. 'Well, I have! I've found them, Mia! It's taken a while, but I started posting on some writing forums and I've found three other people who've been to one of his writing retreats who later found their work published under his name.'

22

Mia stared. She couldn't think of a thing to say, she simply looked between Alex and Tasha.

'Tasha has found Parker's publisher and approached them. They weren't interested at first, but when she gave the names of the other writers and explained that, as a group, they were going to take legal action against Parker, their level of interest seemed to change.'

'Legal action? Tasha, I have no money for a solicitor.' Mia felt bad, shattering all of Tasha's hard work but a lawyer in America would cost thousands, and she simply didn't have the money.

'You don't need it!' Tasha said.

Mia rubbed at her eyes, weariness washing over her. It was all too much, first despair, then hope, then despair again.

'I think Mia needs you to explain the

rest,' Alex said, and Mia could see that he was still smiling.

'One of the other writers is American,' Tasha said.

'I hope that he's rich,' Mia said, dully.

'Actually, no,' Tasha said, with a smile. 'But he approached one of those lawyers that work for nothing and get paid if they win.'

Mia rolled her eyes — great plan! Leave her future in the hands of some dodgy lawyer.

'Anyway,' Tasha said, ignoring Mia's expression, 'the lawyer said that there was no case unless other people could be found with proof.'

'But that's just it, Tasha. I have no proof.'

'You have your notebook, with all your original plans and character sketches. The lawyer said if you can provide that, and anything else you have about your novel, that with the others it should be enough to get the case to court.'

'Just so it can get thrown out? Parker is bound to have a decent lawyer, and if he doesn't, the publishing company will have.'

'That's just it. This has happened to the publishers before and the negative publicity was brutal. The lawyer says he is sure they will want to settle before the case is brought to court.'

'Tasha, this is all amazing, and you've worked really hard — but I'm not really after money.'

Mia tried to look grateful, but everything that Tasha had done was only going to drag out her getting over it, a process that she knew she needed to work through. Although the money would be nice, it would never replace the fact that her book was gone.

'No, you don't get it!' Tasha said, leaping out of her chair. 'They love the book, Mia, and they want to publish it!'

'I know, Parker told me.' Mia had a sudden urge to run away. She knew she hadn't been ready to face anyone yet. The last thing she wanted to do was yell at Tasha, when all she had tried to do was help. Tasha looked at Alex and nodded.

Alex reached out for both of Mia's hands and squeezed them.

'What Tasha is trying to tell you is that they want to publish *your* book, Mia. Your book, with your name on the front cover.'

For the first time in her life, Mia understood how sometimes news, either good and bad, could make a person want to faint. She could see black dots dancing in front of her eyes and the sound of the ocean rushing in her ears. The chattering of the family seemed to dim and she was just about to give into it when she felt Alex shake her.

'Mia?' he asked, concerned. She blinked and felt the dots dim and the ocean disappear.

'I'm dreaming,' she said, since that was the only sensible answer to what had just happened. Alex and Tasha laughed.

'You're not dreaming, silly!' Tasha said, hugging her. 'And you totally deserve this.'

'Tasha, I ... ' Mia didn't know what to say, how to thank her.

'Please,' Tasha said, waving it off. 'You have spent your whole life sorting out my problems. It's about time that I got a chance to help you with one of yours!'

Mia could feel herself start to cry, but they were happy tears this time. She hugged Tasha tightly, whispering, 'Thank you,' over and over again. Then she found herself in Alex's arms being thoroughly kissed by him, before he turned and made an announcement in Greek — although Mia knew that he was telling the family her good news, since they formed an untidy queue to hug and kiss her and congratulate her. When they were finally done, she sought out Alex's arms.

'Is this really happening?' she asked softly.

'Maybe not as you planned, my love, but yes, this is really happening.'

Mia felt sure if she stayed where she was any longer she would fall asleep. Alex's arms held her tightly and from time to time he would kiss the top of her head gently. She marvelled at how different the world looked now, from how it had that morning.

'So what happens next?' she asked, a little muffled by his shirt.

'They will call you in the morning. Tasha wanted to be the one to tell you and I don't think they wanted to argue with her under the circumstances. She is fierce, that little one.'

Mia's eyes sought out Tasha, who was sat next to Tim, sharing a joke with the rest of the family.

'She is. I don't know that I ever noticed that before.'

'Perhaps you underestimate the people in your life.'

Mia felt certain that was a criticism, but then she felt Alex's shoulders gently shake as he laughed; he was teasing.

'It seems I do.' She wiggled far enough away so that she could look him in the eyes. If she was going to apologise then she wanted to do it properly.

'I'm sorry, Alex. I should have listened to you ...'

Alex pressed a finger to her lips.

'I think I gave you reason not to,

my love.'

He looked so solemn that she had to laugh, and he laughed with her. At that moment, Elizabeth brought out the dessert and although Mia had eaten enough to last her several days she couldn't quite resist what could only be considered as Elizabeth's speciality. She managed to sit back in her own chair but Alex kept his arm around her as if he wasn't quite willing to let her go.

'You will remember me when you are a famous author?' he asked, softly, so that only she could hear. Mia laughed and then saw his expression.

'I'm not going anywhere Alex,' she said, and then the full impact of those words struck her. What *was* she going to do? The reason for being in Crete had come to a happy conclusion but she had not given a single thought as to what that might mean for her and Alex. Was she really going to go home now?

She knew that Alex was studying her face but he remained silent. She didn't want to tell him that she hadn't really thought about it. It had seemed so far away and when everything with Parker had happened, it was as if it didn't matter where she was, since her dream, her goal was over.

She felt a gentle kiss on her cheek.

'I was not expecting an answer right now, my love. I know what I want, but you must take the time to decide what it is that you want.'

'I want you,' she said simply, and she knew that it was true.

'Alas, it is not as simple as that, I think,' he said, and smiled, but Mia could see that there was a tinge of sadness in his eyes.

'Maybe it is,' she said, before she could change her mind.

'Mia,' he said, in a manner that was gently scolding, 'you are a planner and you need time to think. Please do not say what you think I want to hear.'

Mia took a deep breath. Alex was right, she was a planner. She had managed her life like that from infant school, but maybe it was time for a change. She had come to Crete with grand plans, none of which had turned out how she had expected. In the past, when her plans had failed, it had seemed like the end of the world. But the truth was, her world was better for all the unplanned things that had happened. She looked again at Tasha who was holding hands with Tim as they shared a private moment together. Life was unpredictable, but that was ok.

'Perhaps Crete has changed me, as Elizabeth said it would,' she said, all of a sudden feeling a little shy.

'How has it changed you?' Alex asked with an innocent expression that didn't really hide his true feelings.

'Well, it is a magical place and I think I have fallen in love with it … ' She looked at him teasingly.

'And? Is there anything else that you have fallen in love with?'

Mia made a great show of thinking but lost it when she felt Alex start to tickle her mercilessly. In fact she would have fallen off her chair if he had not caught her. And so she found herself back in his arms.

'I love you, Alex. Like I have never loved anyone else before.'

'I love you too, Mia, but what will we do?'

Mia looked into the eyes of the man she had fallen in love with and in that moment she knew how Elizabeth had made that decision all those years before. It was easy, really. She loved him, heart and soul. There was no version of her future that she could imagine without him in it.

'Well you can't leave your family, I understand that now. And I wouldn't want you to,' she added, to make sure he knew that was not what she was asking. 'But I can write anywhere,' she continued, with a small smile. 'In fact, Crete seems to be the perfect place for me to write. It's like I've found my muse.'

She leaned in to kiss his cheek so that he would know that she meant him.

'But what about your dreams?' she asked, suddenly remembering the dreams that he had given up.

He shrugged.

'Dreams change, Mia. Sometimes life changes them for us and sets us on a different path, a better path.' He pulled her closer to him and Mia watched as his eyes found Tasha in the crowd that was his family. 'But what of your family? I can't ask you to abandon them, not even for love,' he said, softly, so only she could hear.

There were the sounds of laughter from the end of the table.

'Something tells me they will manage fine without me.'

Alex still looked doubtful.

'Tasha and Tim managed to sort things out on their own. If anything, me interfering all the time just made it harder for them. And besides, I suspect we will see a lot of my family, if Tasha and Tim are anything to go by.'

'Are you sure?' he said, face still serious.

'As sure as Elizabeth was,' she said, with a smile.

Alex continued to study her for a moment and so she smiled and allowed him to work through whatever was going on in his head.

'My father tells me she was pretty sure,' he said, and leaned in for a kiss.

'Well, so am I. And you mother was right, too.'

'Oh?'

'The men on this island have magical powers. Well, one man in particular definitely has.'

Mia put a hand either side of Alex's face and kissed him, melting into his arms. The rest of the family seemed to have finally noticed that something significant was going on and started to cheer and then ask questions. With some reluctance Mia pulled away enough to allow Alex to explain. To explain that they were in love, and they were going to stay together, forever.

We do hope that you have enjoyed reading this large print book.

Did you know that all of our titles are available for purchase?

We publish a wide range of high quality large print books including:
Romances, Mysteries, Classics
General Fiction
Non Fiction and Westerns

Special interest titles available in large print are:
The Little Oxford Dictionary
Music Book, Song Book
Hymn Book, Service Book

Also available from us courtesy of Oxford University Press:
Young Readers' Dictionary
(large print edition)
Young Readers' Thesaurus
(large print edition)

For further information or a free brochure, please contact us at:
Ulverscroft Large Print Books Ltd.,
The Green, Bradgate Road, Anstey,
Leicester, LE7 7FU, England.
Tel: (00 44) **0116 236 4325**
Fax: (00 44) **0116 234 0205**

HEART OF THE MOUNTAIN

Carol MacLean

Emotionally burned out from her job as a nurse, Beth leaves London for the Scottish Highlands and the peace of her aunt's cottage. Here she meets Alex, a man who is determined to live life to the full after the death of his fiancée in a climbing accident. Despite her wish for a quiet life, Beth is pulled into a friendship with Alex's sister, bubbly Sarah-Jayne, and finds herself increasingly drawn to Alex . . .

MIDSUMMER MAGIC

Julie Coffin

Fearing that her ex-husband plans to take their daughter away with him to New Zealand, Lauren escapes with little Amy to the remote Cornish cottage bequeathed to her by her Great-aunt Hilda. But Lauren had not even been aware of Hilda's existence until now, so why was the house left to her and not local schoolteacher Adam Poldean, who seemed to be Hilda's only friend? Lauren sets out to learn the answers — and finds herself becoming attracted to the handsome Adam as well.

DANGEROUS WATERS

Sheila Daglish

On holiday in the enchanting Hungarian village of Szentendre, schoolteacher Cassandra Sutherland meets handsome local artist Matthias Benedek, and soon both are swept up in a romance as dreamy as the moon on the Danube. But Matt is hiding secrets from Cass, and she is determined never to love another man like her late fiance, whose knack for getting into dangerous situations was the ruin of them both. Can love conquer all once it's time for Cass to return home to London?

THE MAGIC OF THORN HOUSE

Christina Green

After the death of her dear Aunt Jem, Carla Marshall inherits Thorn House, the ancient country manor where she spent a happy childhood. But her arrival brings with it fresh problems. She meets and falls in love with local bookseller Dan Eastern — but is he only after the long-lost manuscript of one of Aunt Jem's books, which would net him a fortune if Carla can find it? And her aunt's Memory Box hides a secret that's about to turn Carla's world upside down . . .